Dear Kevin & Mary,
     John, Emily & Henry,
     Who knows who will like
this story? I hope you will find
Margaret and Malcolm as close
to you as they are to me.
          Merry Christmas!
               Love,
               Anne Guerin
               2014

Margaret of Scotland

Anne Guerin

Here are some imaginings of how it might have been,
So that you will read them and say,
"No, it could not have been that way!"
Then go find the things that they first wrote of her,
And speak with her in heaven,
Asking her to tell you how it really was.

authorHOUSE®

AuthorHouse™ LLC
1663 Liberty Drive
Bloomington, IN 47403
www.authorhouse.com
Phone: 1-800-839-8640

Published by AuthorHouse 08/05/2014

ISBN: 978-1-4969-0673-1 (sc)
ISBN: 978-1-4969-0672-4 (hc)
ISBN: 978-1-4969-0671-7 (e)

Library of Congress Control Number: 2014907074

Any people depicted in stock imagery provided by Thinkstock are models, and such images are being used for illustrative purposes only. Certain stock imagery © Thinkstock.

This book is printed on acid-free paper.

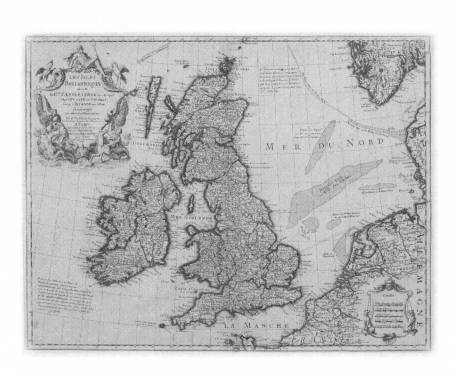

Contents

Prologue

hen, in the Year of Our Lord 1066, William the Bastard of Normandy laid waste the English army at Hastings, many were the survivors who fled. Among these was Edgar, Atheling pretender to the English throne. He, being but fifteen and not altogether forceful, was in the company of his widowed mother Agatha and his two sisters, Margaret and Christina.

With their loyal retainers they took ship and rode the seas up the southeast coast of Scotland, where they broke into the Firth of Forth. They anchored and sent a courier up the path to Dunfermline Castle, where dwelt Scotland's king, Malcolm III Canmore. Then they sat in their ship, awaiting his pleasure.

Some will tell you that the princely family had lost their way and been blown to Scotland by accident. Others say that in fact King Malcolm had invited them. I believe that they had plied their way straight to Dunfermline on purpose, as you shall see.

But this story is not of how they came to Dunfermline, nor is it about Edgar. It is about Edgar's older sister Margaret, then in her young twenties and still unmarried. And here she sits on a November day in the Firth of Forth, with her family and their household in their strong little sea-worn ship, the barely stirring water slapping it gently side to side. Fog swathes them as they sit stilly waiting.

1

The gray was close to her face, and it extended as far as she could see. The gray was soft and damp and smooth. Margaret could feel it rebounding from the slopes on each side of the firth — a much different feeling than the wild, wanton feel of the open sea. Already she felt some reprieve, knowing they had entered this sheltered place. Yet the grayness still bound her. It came in under her clothes and clung to her, tightening the grip of the cold. Would she ever again feel more than cold?

The cold had stolen into her stomach those months ago as she had made that shameful trip with all her family and their retainers, with the great bishops and priests, and with her brother Edgar, heir of Edward Ironside to England's throne, to wait at Berkhampstad for William the Bastard of Normandy and bow their heads before him. To smile sickly in pacification and surrender, and to pass unharmed with eyes averted, from the unhealthy shores of their people to the deck of a ship floating free toward safety. The cold over the water had penetrated her body during all their days of tearing wind and water, and darkness relieved only by gray. It had subsided in the days when the Bishop of Durham gave them shelter, but his fires had never reached her bones.

Now, these days back on the ship, there was never relief from the wet. Under the shelter, where Margaret, her mother, and her sister Christina spent most of their time with their women, they were protected from fresh sheets of water, but mist permeated everything, and their leather slippers were never dry from the three inches of bilge steadily slapping in the bottom of the ship.

Margaret had spent much of her time on deck, helping with all there was to do to run the ship. The distinctions between the work of male and female, of lord and vassal, were much effaced on this small vessel pitched against the great sea. These hours of working together, of teasing and singing, of trying their ingenuity against the elements, of sharing whatever they could cook, had been hours of great freedom and pleasure. Fear even of pursuers or of raiding Northmen left them. Only when she was back in the shelter riding out the time, had Margaret felt the cold and the grayness.

And now, there was no further to travel. They were anchored in the Firth of Forth, holding their place on the silent water, while some of the men went to shore to find the Tower of the Crooked Stream—Dunfermline, castle of the Scots king, Malcolm III.

To be a princess while waiting! It was already long habit in Margaret to bear herself with the dignity of one bonded to her people. So, though the salt of sweat and the salt of the sea mingled old on her skin, though her hair stuck oily to her head and her soft shoes stuck wet to her feet, though her hands and face could not be washed of the smells of smoke and fried fish, she held herself in integrity, sitting tall, breathing the good things that always give joy and strength. She felt the delicateness of the mist and the vigor of the biting air. She listened to the muffled silence. She rode the sway of the ship as a gentle dance. She laughed lightly with her family and fellow passengers. And in these ways she took strength from the Creator of Creation, so that she did not drowse off in the dullness and the long anticipation.

Out of the fog came the lick of an oar dropping water. Regularly, the clear slip and drop, slip and drop of water cut and fallen. Out of the grayness, a darker shape, with more shapes behind it.

The man rowing this first small curragh was not one of their men. He was large and shaggy. He worked his oar powerfully and as though driven. When he lifted his face, she recognized it. Yes, this was the Malcolm she had glimpsed occasionally in the great hall of King Edward, or out in the castle yard, training. The same wild, red hair and wide shoulders; the lithe, powerful movement, and the face, strong-featured, weathered, and, as he came closer she could see, with the penetrating, fierce dark eyes, bright under the heavy brows.

But shaggy! He had ever appeared somewhat unkempt—a man who scrubbed well and put things on straight, but could not bother with fine combing or with keeping his apparel any more in line than it needed to be to get things done. But now! His tangled red hair and beard were longer, and as free as a dog's coat. She saw why they called him *Canmore—Great Head.*

The fur around his shoulders seemed almost raggy. His wool plaid was tied back so he could work, leaving his glistening arms and legs near naked.

He called out to them in English in a voice not unlike a bear's, a voice that came to them warm.

"God give you peace, my guests! I've waited for you too long!"

He pulled himself lightly into the ship, and went first to Margaret's mother Agatha, widow of her murdered father, King Edward Atheling. Then he went to her brother Edgar, and to her and Christina. There was tight clasping of one breast to another, for this had been a flight in great danger, and the man who gave them harbor knew enough of danger and struggle. He had returned not ten years before from his own refuge in the court of Margaret's grandfather, Edward Ironside.

They met Malcolm's son Duncan, a gangly but retiring boy of eight, left alone with his two younger brothers these months ago when his mother Ingeborg had died. Then everyone from the ship was parceled out to one of the small, light Gaelic boats, and it seemed no time until they were ashore. Waiting for them were a group of horses, noble and tough, well but roughly equipped, grazing on some course grass. As the travelers prepared to mount them, they showed their spirit.

"I ask your pardon," offered Malcolm. "We have not many horses for ladies. These horses are not big, but they have the spirit of the devil! Let's see now, who's most gentle?"

By the time he had assigned the gentlest horses to Agatha and Christina and some of the ladies-in-waiting, only true steeds were left. They found willing riders among the good English horsemen, but as Margaret stood still on the ground awaiting her turn, Malcolm looked at her.

"No, I know where you go, Princess Margaret. You'll ride Fire Heart himself! You need his heat, for you're shivering like mercury."

Indeed, crossing in the curraghs Margaret had begun to shiver. All these days of cold she'd stayed firm, but now—What was it? The relief? The warm, strong hand that had helped her from the boat? Now her body would not stop its shaking.

The king—and for sure he was the king, though not so exquisitely robed—bent by his stallion and made a stirrup for her with his hands. There was no question but that Margaret would step up.

How wonderful it felt to swing up onto that powerful back, waiting tensely for who would be master! How free and tempting, after all those days kept in the cup of a boat, to feel the horse's communication under her, and his power, questioning whether it was to be hers.

"And *I* shall ride pillion!" Malcolm cried, and with a light jolt, he had taken the place where usually the woman rode. While Margaret sat tall in some consternation, but not too much after all these days of variability, he spread his ample plaid like a great wing which he folded over her, almost covering her two wet feet. He did not touch her, except where his arms holding the reins grazed hers. He nudged his horse to start.

Malcolm did not smell of salt herring, as many Scots did, but clean. The wool of his plaid carried the mingled scents of horses, leather, smoke, and dampness, mellow and comforting. Though not touching, Margaret could actually feel the heart in his firm chest, and she could feel the strength in his thighs. She could easily have rested her head back on that chest and nodded into his rhythm, but she sat tall within his arms and shivered.

"You do still shiver so, Margaret," he said softly. "We must get you to the fire."

She and the king conversed as they rode along on the rocky path and under the dripping trees—comforting, gentle talk of the things they were seeing and would see.

"How I hope you will like it here, Margaret. It's not so grand as the life you've known, but indeed, my home, too, is grand if you have eyes to see it. I hope you *will* see it."

"How can it not be grand for us, dear King Malcolm? You give your own home for us who have nothing but fear and exile. You must know how grateful we are—how grateful I am."

"Forget it's a refuge, dear lady. You are making a royal visit which I have long awaited, and you are to see and enjoy the best of Scotland."

"I am thinking that, too, sire. I'll take your royal command!"

They rode without speaking. Then Malcolm said,

"I knew today when I saw you that you were Margaret. I remember you as a girl, but it is what I've heard of you now that let me recognize you."

His manner was of genteel distance, but it was too warm.

"Then you know I'm impatient to get to the cloister?" she answered. "As soon as these troubles subside enough, I'll leave your lovely land for the monastery."

"Aye, Margaret, so I had heard," said the king.

Now Dunfermline Castle was before them. Margaret could feel the king's feelings rise as he watched them behold it.

By the time they reached the castle gate, he noticed, "You're not shivering, Margaret."

She had been looking up at him, but she lowered her glance.

"Aye, I am not," she answered.

The gate opened and they entered the castle courtyard. Retainers, all at least as shaggy as their king, came to take reins and carry gear.

nd now, how not to be dismayed? The muck Malcolm had to carry Margaret over to set her on a firm stone! The hall! Almost no light came in from outside. The fire burned like a great eye in the center, and people moving about within were shadowy in the smoke. The rushes on the floor were old and had been pushed mostly into the corners. Hounds slept near the fire or wandered over to greet their master and his guests. Their fur carried pieces of straw they had been sleeping in. Had their coats ever been brushed?

And the hall was almost all there was to the castle. There were workrooms, storerooms, and kitchens; there were rooms in the tower and in the walls meant for defense, but the living was to be done by all in this hall.

King Malcolm himself showed Margaret, Agatha, and Christina a curtained-off area for them, with a cupboard for their belongings. He left them with some of his ladies while he saw to preparations for a great feast. In his enthusiasm he seemed so lonely. How different life must have been when Ingeborg was here and healthy! Though truly, she was a Norsewoman. Her ways of leading a court must have been somewhat different from those Margaret was used to. Their children, too. How had they been when their mother lived? Now, they were quiet and retiring, and stayed more together than with anyone else in the household.

That night the boards were set up on trestles, with many seated around the boards filling one another with stories and laughs while they waited for the king's bounty to fill their stomachs. The confusion was not seemly to Margaret, trained in the courts of Stephen of Hungary and Edward Confessor by Benedictines who led people to seek their place in the order of creation and there to dwell peacefully.

She herself was not much cleaner than when they had arrived, and in all the confusion she felt more her own discomfort and fatigue. But great trenchers of meat were brought in, smoking and steaming and wafting savors she had missed for so long, and all grew quiet, at least until the king's meat was carved, but not long enough for a blessing. Then meat and bread and ale, and even apples that had been stored, were passed freely while all ate their fill. The English visitors took their cue from their hosts. Pausing only for their own silent grace, they served themselves well from all that was offered, eating with their hands and their knives. Sitting close to the king, they showed their good appetite for the fare he offered.

But Margaret and her mother and sister had to hold their hands carefully out of their laps after they had eaten. They did not want to get grease on their skirts, and there were no napkins but the backs of the hounds. Margaret could be as carefree as her hosts in many things, but she would *not* use the fur of a hound!

Now, after the red meat and fresh bread and ale had taken the edge off their discomfort, the ale continued to flow, and the king proposed a toast to them. Others took his lead, answering his toast with more, to him and to them, with an occasional bawdy or battle song. The fire and the breathing and the ale had made them hot, and Margaret wished for a back to her bench to rest through these hours of revelry.

Then some glistening, red-faced laird raised his horn and addressed her with leering eyes in his own Gaelic tongue. Margaret did not understand his words, but whatever he said, it caused King

Malcolm to bring down his own goblet on the table with a crash, his arm slicing full right and left, sending everything on the table to the floor. His sword came out, and he slashed down within a hair's breadth of the toaster's nose and into the wood of the table.

How quickly the hall emptied of those who had come from outside! Those who made their home in the castle hurried quickly to their benches along the walls of the hall. No one touched the boards to clear them or to take them down. The meat that was left, and the bread and ale and fruit, stayed where they were. No one made a long toilette, but all rolled into their blankets and sheepskins, and as it quieted, the hounds stood to the table to find the leavings.

Margaret crawled between the skins she had been shown. The privy was a bit away outside, and the spring for washing, and the great hall doors had been barred shut. She could only lick her greasy hands. She tried to settle into the blankets and thank God for their warmth, but soon the tiny blanket creatures came out to feast. Could she not thank God for this haven? Could she not thank God for their rescuer? The man had felt like strength and music to her, yet he let his whole court rise and fall on his temper. Could she not thank God even for his little creatures that kept her from crying herself to sleep?

But you know, dear God, I really don't have thanks or anything else to give you. Who am I to think of offering myself to you? What shriveled gift am I? Keep me, O Lord. Keep me, O Lord.

3

Two days after they had arrived, the sun burnt through the mist and lifted it into nowhere. From such a fresh, blue sky the sun came cleanly dancing through the whole countryside. It was warming the stones of the building when Margaret came outside early in the morning, and their gray sparkled. The moss on the walls flashed green and living in the air, and the green in the rest of the countryside, though she could scarcely see it over the castle enclosure, she could feel and smell. And all that had been muted in the mist now sang clearly—the clomping and snuffing of the castle animals, the clatter and chatter of the people putting things to rights for the day, the calls of birds, both rough and sweet, and everywhere the thin, ribbony song of autumn breeze.

Malcolm was exultant. He was dressed and clean and had come from the stables before they had sat for their morning bread. He stood in the open door of the great hall, the sunlight behind him, and invited his guests all:

"Today I can show you where you are!

"Hurry, Lady Agatha. Christina, Margaret, Edgar. Bring your court. We're saddling horses for you all. We'll ride out and you'll see what we hid from you at first—land too glorious for you to behold until you'd breathed our strong air!"

The next hours were, indeed, a trip of wonders. Off over the rocky trails into great, green glens and up higher, to what he called the moors—wild, almost moving land, swooping deeply across and up, afire with the fall-reddened brush. No land was unbroken, but always heaving around great rocks and cut with pushing springs and falls. Never did they clop placidly along a mellow path as in England. The air might be the same that blew across that land, but this land did not welcome the air the same. All was rugged and strong, and would never drowse. Even the cliffs of Dover would seem bland and worn, Margaret thought, after seeing these gray crags and drops over which King Malcolm so joyously guided them.

He led and then he gradually dropped back, engaging her mother and brother, and she and her sister, too, and also each of their retainers, to get their impressions of the land that had given him his blood. Then he would ride behind them for some time, and next he would have them stop so they could appreciate a certain sweep or a particular waterfall. Sometimes he would call out to a woman working in her yard and ask her to bring her children to meet his guests, or to show them the wool on her loom. He might stop a man with his cart and ask him about his wife and his family and his winter seeding. He stopped some men fishing in a big stream to show them their catch—not only the collection itself, but each type of fish native to his land, that they might value its unique beauty.

Margaret could see that the land was glorious. She knew the air was pungent and clean, like cider just beginning to turn. She knew that she, too, should exult just to breathe it. She could see easily the pride and glory Malcolm took in this land, a land that would not let one be anything but young. But she saw and she smelled and she listened as one confined, looking out. What she saw could not get in and raise her heart.

She begrudged her uncouth horse, not trained to the niceties of a lady. She felt the lumps and the roughness and the sweat—yes, the old sweat in her own hair and clothes. She would not pick up the simple song Malcolm sang, a lay made to be joined easily by all. She rode quietly, pretending not to know that their host was inviting her and all to break into his traveling song.

She was ashamed, especially seeing that she was the cosseted guest not only of this king, but of the King of Creation, seeing beauty that should make one weep. But she felt that if she opened her mouth to sing, she would croak.

Now, after riding through heather and broom and up along rocks, and then along the cliffs and down the river to the sea beach itself, King Malcolm was determined to take them in under some sunny pines to follow the trail to a small loch. They could never rest content today, he was sure, if they could not behold just one of these deep, clear, cold lakes.

Why should Margaret be feeling the time, and so anxious to be finished? From this great, sunny, breezy country she had only to go back to the dim, smoky hall.

They came over the forested mountain and down to the wide, smooth stretch of blue water. What Malcolm was saying of the loch she didn't follow. But now he was urging them to take off their shoes and walk at least to their ankles into the stinging water. Margaret looked to her mother and saw that she herself was taking off her shoes.

Why was she not thrilled? Here in Scotland they were allowed to do many of the things they would have had to forego according to courtly etiquette in her former homes. The hard, cold water was not enough for her feet. She wanted to keep wading and to swim out, out, never far enough or deep enough.

At last they were on their way back to Dunfermline. Again the king was moving up and down the line of riders, wanting to hear their pleasure. He rode next to Margaret, but their words were few and forced.

When they arrived in the courtyard, Malcolm came to help her down from her horse.

"You didn't like it did you, Princess Margaret?"

"Oh, my lord, it was most lovely! Fairer country I have never seen."

"No, Margaret, you were never pleased. What did you not like?"

"Oh, I liked everything, Your Highness. You are so attentive to us. You have shown us loveliness that only you know. You gave me such a good horse, and the country is very lively!"

"You are not happy, Margaret."

She was afraid to try to speak.

"Margaret," said the king, "if you could have one thing right now, what would make you truly smile?"

Where was her breath? How could she hold her chest?

"A bath, Your Majesty," and the sobs took over, shaking her and rocking her as a princess should never let herself be shaken.

"A bath, dear Margaret? A bath is what you'd like? Aye, you shall learn what a bath the Scots can give you."

And she did, and her mother, too, and her sister. And Edgar, and everyone who had come with them.

It was such a bath, too! One you could sit in, and hot, with good soap, and good rinsing, and somehow, even a drying cloth that was truly clean. Now her hair blew clean and light in the breeze, and on her clean skin she put clean clothes from her trunk.

The washing of bodies began the washing of clothes. Then the king had them washing and cleaning not only their own possessions, but those provided for them in the hall.

"I do know," he told Margaret, taking her aside, "when one has been clean and had order, it is hard to do without it. We have had better here, too, but with Ingeborg sick, and then gone, if we had peace and warmth and enough to eat I was glad enough. So often I have to leave to fight, or someone's pounding at our gate, or we have sickness, and it's hard enough to keep us all fed. My people get lazy, and I hate to order and nag and complain. It's easier to believe that they're doing what they can.

"The skins and blankets—they're crawling, aren't they?"

He went to her mother and asked if she would direct the cleaning of the bedding. There began such days of cleaning and purifying not only of bedding, but of everything in the hall—the walls and the floors, and even the rafters under the roof. Then came the scullery, and Agatha wanted to arrange things better for babes and their mothers.

As guests, they had been able only to accept graciously whatever form of hospitality they were given, but when the king invited them—aye, *begged* them to help oversee the cleaning, then that great pleasure was their duty. It made all of them feel better to be useful to their host. And Malcolm was wonderful at raging and roaring with his servants so that not one of them could raise an eyebrow that *perhaps* Queen Agatha might at *all* have been longing to oversee this very task.

Yet—Margaret smarted when she thought of how it had all begun, and no doubt the news had flitted quickly, from the moment it had happened. The princess of England had asked the king of Scotland for a bath!

So began a work and a place for Agatha and her children in Malcolm's household. Agatha respected all who had been conducting the house, and gave them prerogatives, but gently she raised their discipline, so that they took fierce pride in making their king's house one that excelled in all things.

4

The fair weather held until St. Andrew's Day, and one of the lairds invited Malcolm and his guests to celebrate it with their village. They rode over in the darkness of early morning. The laird, all his household, and all the village waited formally for the royal arrival. They led them to the hut-like church where they would celebrate St. Andrew's Mass.

But, though the king's party were the first except the priest to enter the church, the place seemed hardly in readiness for such a day. The priest was just now lighting worn-down candles, which were the only light in this windowless building. It could not smell exactly rotten or dirty, for the strong cold freshened it. But the smells were of earth and mildew, and the candlelight fell on surfaces dull and dusty. The floor, of packed earth, had not been pounded or strewn with reeds for many Saturdays. The ladies' skirt hems must surely be picking up cobwebs and rat droppings. There were set up handsome chairs for the princely families, but Margaret could hardly force herself to take a chair when she saw that the altar for her Lord was nothing more than a rough slab, and the priest did not even dust it before he spread the white cloth.

There was not room either for all the people. The courtly people must sit in privilege while many of the others crowded outside the door. And being left outside did not seem to offend them much, the air being fresher there, and the long mumblings of the Mass easier to bear in conversation with friends.

Aye, she felt close to the stable in Bethlehem when Father raised the white host. Heaven and earth joined like resounding cymbals through the universe, and could any of them hear it? Nothing prepared for him, nothing proclaiming him, but the hearts of children and of angels!

Oh, Lord, I am not worthy that you should enter under my roof. Only say the word and my soul shall be healed.

After the Mass came the village traditional feast. It revolved around chiefs showing generosity and vassals showing homage, with the exchange of gifts of animals to be butchered and shared. There was an order in what should be done and who should do it. All were solemn and ready, as one might have hoped they would have been for the Mass. All for this slitting of throats and slicing of carcasses and wiping of grease! And how the pale, famished eyes looked at that flesh soon to roast and drip juices and satisfy their longing for good, red meat!

Trying to get the spirit of the festivity made Margaret stand back from herself.

I scorn these people's feast. How would the feasts I delight in look to them? The fairs of goods I so value, the meals with such meticulous observance of "gentle" ways to feed one's face and blow one's horn? Is there anything more to my festivities than to theirs?

After all were full and merry, these Scots showed their royal guests ways to caper that knocked the abstinence right out of them. Their game of *gouf (golf)* took skill both of body and of mind. It was nothing but batting a stone across the land with a shepherd's crook, but dropping the stone precisely in the small hole cut for it in the ground required fine-tuned sighting, and good play with the crook and the wind. The laird opened up the whole countryside for this game, so that the players were soon chasing stones down ravines, over stumps, and away from ponds and bogs. Women played as well as men, and children chased along, sighting lost stones, cheering and coaching. Margaret found the quiet Duncan close by her side, teaching her to be a champion. Nobles and common people found themselves bandying one another, for this game overlooked bloodlines for skill.

Never in England or on the continent could Margaret have been tearing along so freely. The challenge of the game caught her up. By the time they were all back to the village green, she felt she'd been lifted into the sky to see the world.

Then the men began to dance. These were warriors' dances— Gillie Callum, the sword dance, and Malcolm's dance of the stag. Folk said you would never see the true soul of these dances unless you were there at the triumph of battle, when the victors broke spontaneously into dancing for joy.

Gillie Callum was danced over two crossed swords: that of the enemy and the bloody one that slew him, often with the enemy's severed head balanced on the point where the swords crossed. The stag dance, or *fling* was one Malcolm had first danced when they had conquered MacBeth in 1054 near Dunsinane. Now the dance was danced everywhere in Scotland, especially in the Highlands. Placing his battle shield, the eighteen-inch-round *targe* with its six-inch center spike on the ground with the spike pointing up, Malcolm stepped on top of it, raised his arms aloft to represent a stag's antlers, and danced light and high. In snapping-quick patterns he leapt, his feet never sliding from the shield nor touching the spike, and his eyes gazing high and far, back to that moment of avenging his father and retrieving the glory of Dunchada. On the village green it was a dance of alacrity and joy in strength, carrying Margaret's heart. But she hoped never to see it or any such dance danced at the scene of battle.

Women, too, had their dances, which Margaret watched until she could learn them better. They, too, displayed skill and strength and stamina, such as a man might look for in a wife. Then men, women, and children fell into the lines and circles that anyone could learn, snatching Margaret with them. They danced until they had to sit, and then they danced again. They danced until they had no breath, and they found more breath and danced again. Margaret kept close to the children and the maids. Evening was falling, and a woman looking toward the monastery need not get too close to men in high spirits.

5

ere was Margaret, daughter of Edward Atheling and sister of Edgar, supplanted king of England, more than twenty years old yet still unmarried, come to shelter with Malcolm III MacDuncan, Chief of Chiefs of all the Scottish clans. To stay for how long? Did she have her whole life to tour the world for interesting sights? When had she been where she belonged?

She had first opened her eyes in Hungary, near Mecseknadasda, in the house of King Stephen, her uncle. Her father had been sent to King Stephen's protection as an infant, when Cnut took the throne left by Edward's father, Edmund Ironside. He had grown up always looking to return to England to fulfill his father's legacy. Though he knew only Hungary, and counted himself lucky to be in that golden court, yet the yearning to get to his life's work lay under all he did. In the peace and prosperity of Stephen's court he learned arts and sciences such as he would hardly have known in England. The learned priests, monks, and nuns came from their peaceful monasteries to the palaces to teach even the children their ways.

Now that Margaret was grown, she often thought of how it must have been for her father—living his gratitude to his hosts, making himself useful, and yet certainly feeling he would not truly be living until he was with the people for whom he was born.

Yet he did not hold out for a Saxon wife. The lovely Agatha satisfied his heart. She was of the line of the Holy Roman Emperors, a fair and intelligent woman, well- educated, and sensitive to the needs of this royal exile. Even though Hungary and England were far from each other in more than miles, the marriage of Edward and Agatha was not so unusual in those times of allying distant realms by marriage.

But if Edward had salvaged any English ideas of how to raise children, he must have put most of them aside, for Margaret was raised according to the lights of continental life. Her mother had strong experience of how a royal child should be educated, and when the tiny girl was still tow-headed, she had the graceful Benedictine nuns teaching her. These women were in many ways as close to her as her mother. They had a sobriety, but yet a wild sparkle. They constantly drew her up taller, expecting her to learn every skill that a good queen should have. First, she must know how to do all that she might ask a servant to do—her own toilette, the making and care of clothes and house furnishings, the provisioning and the cooking and the overseeing of the table. She must become a skilled horsewoman, both for conveyance and for entertainment, and she must learn a horse's needs. She must learn art and music, and to read. Daily she would study, and then discourse with her teachers and with her parents. She was young when she could read the Scriptures, in Latin and in Greek, and she was meditating on the Fathers of the Church before she reached the age when most women married. She must learn all the ways of courtesy and diplomacy. Even from early childhood, she must bear herself with the dignity people deserve from their leaders.

These obligations could have oppressed her, except for the joy and light of those who taught her. It was true that she and her sister and brother were not allowed to caper as freely as a peasant, but they felt a freedom in their souls that assuaged the hunger to be free in custom. How often their teachers reminded them that the Creator of Creation was their Father—Abba, Papa! That he *delighted* in them! That he held them close, tenderly. They might not often feel it, for his love was too powerful for humans to understand, but he had put all creation into their hands. It was only for them to learn his ways and his times, and the fullness of all he had entrusted to them would show itself. So convinced were they of his love and of their absolute freedom that they could be patient to wait for its fullness.

All the arts Margaret learned seemed to be born in church. Her first reading was in the sacred Scriptures. Her first singing was of the psalms of the Sisters' office. Her finest sewing was the rich needlework for priests' vestments and the accessories of the Mass. The beginning of etiquette was before God in the church.

This was the way of Christendom—well established in Central Europe, and not quite as consistent but still esteemed in the North. The rulers of each people were so closely associated with the Church that the customs of noble houses took their pattern from the customs of monasteries. Priests and consecrated men and women were considered essential members of a court. Every noble castle day began with the Eucharist. The external religious customs could be depended on. Whether the soul of these customs thrived or not was a matter of individual freedom. At least the spirit had a constant physical reminder of God's point of view.

So Margaret, Christina, and Edgar grew up close to nuns and priests and masters who loved them as they trained them strictly. With all the skills they mastered, they stood freer within themselves. To Margaret these days were dear. The people who cared for her she loved and treasured.

How her father had kept himself at peace all those years, Margaret now marveled. To her he had seemed always busy with what needed to be done. What had it been? Somehow keeping his balance with each of King Stephen's successors, training with his men, yes, and caring for the poor with his wife Agatha and their children. This work absorbed him, yet, especially in the years of malicious discord following Stephen's death, how it must have chafed him to be always a guest! It was practice in a virtue of any good king—to know that, even in his own kingdom, he is but the guest of God.

How much time had her father spent in communicating with England? Certainly he had good friends who kept him regularly informed, and who carried out his instructions.

Then came the message from the English *Whitan*, the king's council, summoning Edward to return as their king. Twelve years before, the English had taken the throne from the sons of Cnut and returned it to one of their own, Edward the Confessor. He had proved himself "a lover of peace who protected his kingdom by peace rather than by arms." Yet so did he love God's peace that Edward had vowed virginity in God's service. His council called Edward the Exile back to secure the English succession.

Margaret did not remember the courier from his arrival, but from tracing the great change back to him. How quiet her father had become, and her mother, too. Her father's was a tense quietness, but somehow one of lightness and release. Her mother's feelings Margaret did not sense as well—only that she became vigorous and methodical in action. For her mother's feelings were bound tight with the bands of duty. What natural feelings could she have had but of impending separation from all that was familiar and dear to her? Yes, with her mind she knew this was the fulfillment they had been awaiting. With her heart she must have known joy, too, in her husband's relief. But she had little more to impel her to England than love of her husband and of God. Besides the prospect of being a queen to an alien country, she had to face the easy possibility of violence to her husband. There were those who had called to him, and there were those who were hostile.

For a ten-year-old girl the trip north had been adventure. Clanking along with the line of travelers, each day through new country, they escaped the usual schedule of work and study. They heard long, colorful stories and sang hours of songs with those who rode beside them. They met so many different people and saw new customs. They were welcomed at an array of castles by new friends. Sometimes they camped in tents. The long hours they spent aboard ship, though rough and dirty, were lyrical, borne by wave and wind.

But any wonder or anticipation she may have felt on that trip was stiffened numb that morning soon after they had begun their life with Kind Edward. The night before, her father had taken so ill. Never would she forget him falling even before he could get from the hall where they dined, retching and shuddering and grabbing himself together in great spasms. Never would she forget that night she had spent trying to obey her mother's admonishment, "Go to sleep. It is nothing. You will see him in the morning," and the morning, so blue with dark, when Agatha touched her on the shoulder and lifted her cover, beckoning her silently to come.

Even now she could see his still, yellow face in the candlelight, his skin seeming to be covered in wax. She could yet feel his forehead as she had pressed hers to it. All the warmth was gone, and the movement in brain and blood completely stopped. She had been so sure that he must revive soon. Until now, it had been his life that pushed hers. Yet she knew that the man was no longer in his body. Even years later, that moment of grasping reality appalled her. Before they even had their bearings in England, all her family's uprooting and traveling mocked them—left them homeless in a country they proclaimed to be theirs.

And with that great, crushing wave of sorrow slowly bearing down, came also the chill behind her neck that would never leave. What had caused her father's death was not a passing contagion, though no one would speak of it. This was the work of nightshade. And whose work was it, of all the cheery members of the court?

With the great emptiness where all had been daughterhood, delight, hope, and a place in the future, came also the full experience of the psalm: "Put not your trust in princes, in men in whom is no salvation."

Agatha kept a retainer in the kitchen—yet how could he notice every hand that lightly passed over a dish with a spray of powder? King Edward never let Agatha or her children go unattended—but what if the very liegeman she trusted proved to be her betrayer?

So a sweet maturity had grown in Margaret. If she were not to live always with a chilling draft at the back of her neck, if she were to know chainless freedom, then Margaret must lay all concern for her life over to God. Of course she would judge friendship as shrewdly as she might; of course she would appreciate those who attended to her safety. But really, during a few months of asking God, care for her life dried away, and she knew only his firm and sure hand, the hand of him who loved her and counted every hair of her head. She enjoyed every new friend. She enjoyed every walk and every ride a-horseback into the wide countryside. She enjoyed every feast, and the good food and drink. She slept well and deep.

In truth, Edward the Confessor gave them security and a rich life in his court. He gave them the easiest court to call home, for Edward's court was livened by the love of God. Thus they found there more the things that all men share than the things in which people differ.

New, kind nuns resumed Margaret and Christina's training. A mistress of maidens looked after all their needs. Margaret took up the delicate needlework in gold for the Liturgy that was renowned throughout Europe as *Opus Anglicum—the work of angels*. Her mother Agatha adapted to the English way of life, sometimes not easily, and sometimes transforming it to a better way she knew. She and King Edward saw to Edgar's education for kingship. Never would they travel far from England as her husband had done, dwelling too distant from his land to return to his throne. Edgar would grow daily close to the strong men who would support him, and learn the ways and the needs of those he must soon govern. That that purpose soured in Edgar himself did not deter Agatha and her advisors from persevering in all that they had begun.

For Margaret, as for her family, there could be no looking back to Hungary. It had been only the foster home for a family dedicated to serve England. Whenever they felt sad or empty, Margaret's mother taught them, they must look not back to what they remembered, but around them to those God gave them now. This was easier for the children than it was for their mother. Their father's blood in them sought their Saxon relatives.

But Margaret's true home was the Eucharist, which was indeed the home of Edward's reign. From the early hours of morning she encountered companions in solitude when she came to the dark chapel to bring her soul in tune for Christ's Mass. They knelt or sat in silence, watching with their Lord for the dawn. Then the chaplain would intone the psalms of Lauds, and they would sing those prayers of the Church reaching toward the Eucharist. Then came that great Sacrifice of the Lord. She returned to that chapel at times throughout the day, often finding others there adoring their Lord. Then it was easy to know that all they did, small or great, was adoration.

.   Edward could not have enough visitors to help to explain the reign of God. Though his soul was a child's, demanding nothing of God, he loved God so that he wanted to use every way of pursuing his mystery. So scholars and men and women of prayer were always coming, for an evening or for a season. All who cared to could learn from them. Margaret found such satisfaction, and hunger, too, conferring with these men and women. They became her dear friends. Since many of them were leaders in Church and civil life, their concerns were not only for the things of God, but for God's desires for his people, and of the battles near and far over who should lead them. Lanfranc, the Bishop of London, became her confidant. Having a natural trust in his integrity and understanding, Margaret also put her trust in him as a priest of God.

And so Margaret was used to finding her home in God rather than in any place. Still she felt exile in Edward's court, because a calling had risen in her heart to go straight to God and live all for him, and so for her people. As always, she must ride the waves of politics, so that each time she had been close to leaving for the monastery, the situation of state made it impossible. The crossing over of William from Normandy had swept away any hope of entering a house of prayer in England very soon. So when she saw that her family must leave the country, she was not dismayed but hopeful. Once in some other land, she would be free to follow her vocation.

Then her mother and her advisors had seized on the invitation of Malcolm to come to his castle in Scotland. Though it was beyond the borders of William's realm, yet it still was of a piece with the English island. They would not have to yield as much as they had when Edward Atheling had been spirited to Hungary. Here, close to the borders, Edgar could bide his time. Malcolm had offered to help him when the moment came to challenge William the Norman.

Besides her doubt that any scheme would ever draw more from Edgar than to follow falteringly where he was led, Margaret was taken aback that they had chosen a refuge where there was not a monastery available for a woman like her. As their flight had begun and they rode toward the coast where the ship waited to carry them free, sitting in the saddle she had waited quietly on her Lord. The pure air blew her face; the last leaves and grasses moved in the air. The horses kept up their steady walk, the leather creaking and the fastenings jangling. Hoping to draw the least notice, the party spoke only when necessary, and softy, so she could listen easily for God. How many beautiful sounds he gave her from his small creatures who could not but live his way! Whether the sun fell upon her or the clouds dropped water, what she had was this gracious silence.

Hours passed.

Well, my dear Lord, you must have a fling in mind for me. I covet the quiet world enclosed in walls, and you take me out to the land of the Scot! Such a wild country I never thought I'd see. All right, let them show me around. Show me why you love them! I'll carry their wildness with me when at last my Sisters close the grate. Maybe it's not a milk-toast nun you want me to be.

Now that they dwelt at Dunfermline, Margaret felt it quite barren of spiritual friendship. But even if the chapel was a neglected closet, the Mass was celebrated there daily in its truth. When she came to the chapel, she united herself with all the unseen angels and saints around her, and with all those in far distant places so close to her in the Eucharist. Now her discourses were in pure faith and in spirit. Now she took those precious books she had brought with her, the Scriptures most of all, and pored over them slowly, still finding infinite food. And for companionship in the Spirit, she of course had her sister Christina and her dear mother. How she relied on Agatha for wisdom in what their way should be in the house of Malcolm!

Did Malcolm notice how often now someone knelt in his chapel? He, too, was up early in the morning, and often he sought his guests, wanting to know they were happy with him. Did he raise his eyebrows at this tall Princess Margaret flitting so often to the place of prayer? One thing he did was to happen in more often himself. He came now to Mass daily, as a good king should, and sometimes he came to the quiet chapel when one of them was there, and knelt or sat still for a short trial.

This Malcolm—was he a true Scotsman? Ah, when she had seen him in the years he had taken refuge in Edward the Confessor's court, he looked so. Wild and woolly were they not known to be? *Canmore* they called him, *Great-head*. Was it because of his great rusty mane, or because he naturally led? Many of the clans in the Highlands hardly claimed him, because he would ally with anyone if he saw it useful. The deepest feeling of those people of the North was loyalty to their clan. They feared not for their lives—either that they be killed or that they lose all and starve. Their word was their bond, and their pride was in pure loyalty. (Strange, though, what this purity of clans was. Were they Picts? They had once been. Were they Celts? Were they Gaels? Had not the Scoti left Greece and passed through Egypt to come here and make their home? Indeed Norsemen had been among them for two hundred years, and who was not a little Norse?) But each person could tell you his clan, and the purity of his descent. And if he and his people could live unconquered until they died, what could be a more beautiful life?

Malcolm was of this new breed that saw not so much who you are as how you live. People talked of whether it was power he wanted or peace. But if he saw that he could quiet one threat, or extend one realm, he would ally with those who would help him. Thus he had returned from his exile and with the help of the English had conquered and slain MacBeth, who had slain his father Duncan. Thus he had married a Norsewoman, Ingeborg, the daughter of the Earl of Orkney, the Norse stronghold off the coast of Scotland.

People had said both that Malcolm was a great swaggerer and that he had a heart for the smallest person. So Margaret had not been unprepared for anything she had seen of him since coming to Dunfermline. She herself was not of a sure opinion about him. One thing she could see, and that was how it was that he drew an ally or put spirit into a horde of fighting men. He was a winning man. He had such an urgency of good about him. In his presence, you were sure he was right, and that he would find better ways for you than you would for yourself.

How would his life have been with Ingeborg? Margaret could not help but think of these Norsemen as *Vikings—Raiders.* How many times she had prayed with her people the three-hundred-year-old prayer, "From the wrath of the Norsemen, O Lord, deliver us."

And yet, the name *Norman* meant nothing more than *Norseman.* Normans had developed a richness that was the envy of the continent.

But were these people of Orkney not more barbaric than even the Picts and Gaels? Would Ingeborg have considered herself free to talk with her husband as a friend? What kind of a household would she have conducted? Did she know about washing? About health and medicine? What did she know of courtesy?

Never would Margaret have dared to let another know that she thought these thoughts. She often asked Ingeborg in heaven to indulge her.

Luckily you have a great heart now, Ingeborg. Do not take affront at my prejudice. You will admit that by the time you had been gone a few months, not much was left of your household!

Their children were quiet and seemed lost, as those left without their mother must be. They seemed tough, too, whether from their upbringing or in defense, now that they were so alone. Malcolm gave them affection, but he held himself from them. He could show them such anger!

Malcolm's brother Donald—*Bane* they called him, *the Fair*—had not come down to Dunfermline from the Highlands since the Athelings had arrived. Malcolm spoke of him with affection. They had fought together to overthrow MacBeth and return the kingship to their father's house. Yet the caution with which Malcolm and his friends spoke of his brother carried a sense that Donald might not be so much held by affairs in the North as distancing himself from Malcolm. Did he not see Scottish kingship the way Malcolm did? Was he merely jealous of his brother?

The man to whom the brothers owed MacBeth's defeat was Malcolm's good friend MacDuff. He it was who had placed the crown on Malcolm's head at Scone, and Malcolm had made him Earl of Fife, where he had the power of a king. Often did he come to Dunfermline. *He* was the man who seemed like Malcolm's brother.

Who of the Scots failed to notice that this Edgar whom Malcolm had invited to shelter with him brought two handsome, marriageable sisters? Did they consider that the Athelings might think of Malcolm as no more than the chief of a crowd of Gaelic chiefs? In fact, rumor wafted that it was Margaret he had set his heart on. It stung Margaret that even her mother was not averse to such whisperings. Did her own mother take so lightly her long-detained sacred purpose?

But why should it sting? This knowledge she had in her heart did not rise or fall with the thoughts of others. It was from God. If he called her, he would give her her chance. She had only to keep her eyes open.

6

 ow the dark came sooner each day, and with it the chill reached deeper. Used to a life of flight, Agatha and her family did not live looking toward better days. They lived best, they found, if they took up life where they were, as though they had settled in for good. Then, when indeed they moved on, they left satisfied.

They began their day as in all the noble houses of Christendom, with Mass in the castle chapel. This was a custom that had come with the early missionaries, but at Dunfermline it was little more than an expected practice. The chaplain, obliged to offer the Mass daily, got it taken care of at dawn as a good chaplain should, but he was not used to a crowded chapel. Nor was he used to having five or six people silently praying there when he first carried in his candle in the morning, and staying after Mass in thanksgiving. The chapel felt more human breath than perhaps it ever had. Malcolm himself strode in now and then to see what there might be to this bent for worship.

The family resumed such studying as they could. Though they had no resident nuns or scholars as they had been used to, they had the Scriptures and other books which they had brought. They had their study hours each day.

Since that first great cleaning, King Malcolm leaned toward Agatha's help as much as might not offend his faithful staff. The year since losing Ingeborg had left the household at loose ends, and the king looked to Agatha to reestablish prosperity. She, in turn, was glad to be able to contribute, and to have work to do. She brought in her own steward, Bartholomew, and worked respectfully with all in the household, firm in the authority she'd been given, but seeking always to know first the way things had been done until now, and to ask advice. Her son and daughters shared in all that must be done. Edgar went with young Duncan to learn his duties. Christina began to work closely with the clothes supplier. Margaret joined the provisioner of kitchen and banquet hall. She worked next to the cooks and scullery folk, learning the way things were done and listening to the talk.

"There, you knead it roughly, see. A little more oats to your hands so they don't stick. Aye, squeeze it and smooth it until it blisters. A little more like that.

"There! Now you've got your dough! Taste it. Taste the salt? And the lard, not too much; a little water to bind meal and grease.

"Now, you roll it and pull it on the stone so it's round and flat— flat as you can make it without breaking it. Now, throw a little meal on that stone we've got hot, and put your cake on it. Watch your sleeves!

"See there? You've made a bannock!

"You see how we got our stone just so hot? Watch yourself when we turn over the cake. It'll be cooked so nice, and still hardly brown. Throw a little meal on it before you turn it. Aye, you'll turn a few more before you get the feel."

Indeed, they were beautiful bannocks they had made, and the old cook was pleased.

"You've got a good hand there, my queen—almost like a real woman!"

"Haggis! Will you make haggis with me? You must come to my brother's house when they make it. Will you come, dear lady? For you can't make true haggis in the kitchens of the great. It's from the land. You must come to a poor house to make good haggis."

So Margaret came to see the inside of many a home. Whenever she could, she went with Malcolm's steward, or *mormaer*, as they called him, to inspect the stock, the farms, and the stored harvests. And what Scots house did not have its Saxon bondsman, fled from England and held to serve, almost like a beast? How did her fellow Saxons look at her, she living the exile of nobles?

It was Advent, so bleak, though with the thrill of Christmas in the air. As she went visiting, Margaret sensed less the joy of Christmas than the pall of winter. Often she found a family already stretching thin what they had to live on. She would tell these people to come to the castle when they were in need. Next, she was asking the mormaer to bring more from storage. Before Christmas had come, he was having to ask the king to purchase more supplies.

At first Malcolm took this news belligerently. How were they cheating him? Who was slacking; who wasting their stores? ... It was the tall, fair princess from England? Oh, she'd not been here two months and she had passed out everything in his cellars? Yet he hadn't seen that their feasts were that much more robust! ... Oh, she'd taken over the almonry? (Every great house had its almoner for those who came begging.) And she took the liberty to invite whom she fancied?

But he said nothing to Margaret. Instead he came often near to the door where the poor came for alms, and watched the activity now grown quite lively. Almost always he found Margaret there. And, he had to admit, no one he saw taking parcels looked as though what he was given would cause him to overeat.

It expanded Malcolm's feeling as king to see these subjects of his so cared for, and he enjoyed the twist of his lightweight beneficiary so happily handing out all she could find of his reserve.

"Surely it can't be dangerous to feed hungry people," he said. "Procure what she asks for, but see that Princess Margaret oversees giving it out."

So Christmas came, not so much full of tender nostalgia as of the hard work that brought Mary and Joseph to the cave at Bethlehem.

7

n Christmas Day, Margaret, with her mother and sister, held infants and wondered that their God had been one of these. Folk had come for the morning Mass, and stayed to break their fast at Dunfermline castle. Margaret had walked among them and called aside mothers whose babes seemed frail. These were her special care each day, but especially on Christmas. She bathed one's mattered eyes, and washed and oiled his tiny body, mottled with white and crusty splotches, and thought:

Did you, Jesus, have these things growing on you, too? You were poor. Could Mary and Joseph always keep you as shining as they wanted you to be? Ah, but today is your birthday, dear Jesus! You came whole and smooth, pink and tender and not yet sick. You are within this sweet child, Jesus. You let me hold you newborn today.

It was full midmorning when people began to move out of the castle gates to return home. Margaret held some of them back—twenty of them.

"Spend Christmas with us!" she invited. "Come and we'll see what we do!"

King Malcolm had gone down to the stables and she found him there.

"My lord," she asked him, curtsying respectfully, "What is your custom here on Christmas Day? What do we do here now?"

"Now?" he said. "I'm thinking of the bed, aren't you? That Mass at midnight has finished me."

The color rose in Margaret's face.

"Ah, I'm thinking a nap, too," she answered. "We'll rest, and afterward we can make merry."

She hastened back to the hall and settled her newly invited guests on benches with blankets before she lay with relief in her own sheepskins.

When she woke, the light was dulling toward night. Margaret washed in cold water and redid her hair in smooth twines with red satin ribbon. She fastened the red wool dress she had worn for Mass with two small brooches of red stone set in gold. She found her mother to ask about festivities for Christmas night, but Agatha sent her to the king.

"How do we celebrate Christmas night at Dunfermline?" she asked him.

There she stood before Mael Colum, sprightly though almost as tall as he, in the soft red dress, her fire-gold hair wound away from her glowing face with red ribbons. He searched her face a little with his dark eyes and hesitated.

"Do you celebrate Christmas night?" he asked. "Then how shall we celebrate Christmas night?"

So Margaret went for her mother and family, and some who had become friends, to make up a Christmas celebration. They went to the reserves they had brought in their trunks, and brought out packs of raisins and dried citron, and a small cask of strong, sweet wine—enough for a little after dinner. They found a fine, colored banner to hang above the king's table. They laid out some clothes and linens, somewhat worn but colorful and graceful, that might become beautiful costumes. Then Margaret cast about in whatever places she thought of for bits and pieces that might catch the imagination for drama.

They called together all the folk about the castle.

"Tonight," Princess Margaret told them, "we shall have charades of the Infant King! Each of us will play the part of one of those who came to his stable. You must play it well, but keep us fooled! Will these clothes help you to dress your parts? Now, we must practice before dinner!"

Soon all the props were taken, and people were searching about the castle for what they had not yet found, and going off into corners to rehearse by themselves.

At dinner they began toasts to Christ's birth, and Margaret and Christina brought out their harps. They sang carols, and then each took his turn playing some personage or creature who had attended on the Christ Child. Servants were kings and royalty were donkeys. These people who rubbed elbows each day hardly recognized one another in assumed guise—except that they *did* so much recognize one another that before they were through, all were weak with laughter.

Before the gaiety could end, some of the king's men must play their horns and pipes for a final dance—men, women, children, and all!

Next year, thought Margaret, they must prepare better for the ChristMass itself. But next year she would not be here! Easter, then. Six ladies now were working on an Easter stole and altar cloths. Their skill would soon be fine enough to start a chasuble of white and gold. More than that they would not finish by Easter. But she and her mother had sent to France for other fine cloths to decorate the church.

The festivity that people here looked for came in the following week—the ancient Hogmanay, bringing in the New Year. The whole house must be cleaned, their mormaer informed them, and all that was spoiling or rancid must be thrown out. Creditors, humble though they be, appeared each day, reminding the king of his debts, for he would not want to be found owing a debt by the last midnight of the year.

On the night itself, the revelry originated more in the villages than from the house of the king. But Dunfermline, too, had its roaring bonfire in the castle yard, and its tables ready to provide for merry guests. Some of the young men running about the countryside wearing cattle hides came to the castle gates, carrying their smoking brands and seeking their customary beating. In the meantime, the pitch of merrymaking around the fire warmed toward that hour when the new year was to overcome the old. Hugs and kisses were free. *Great Love Day* was coming!

Margaret met many of the evening's guests and raised her glass a few times, but she did not stay up until the horns sounded at midnight. Thankful this night for the curtain they could draw around their beds, she left it to the others to welcome the *First Footer*, the dark man who should step first across their threshold after midnight, bearing the gifts of prosperity.

How could it be, she thought, that Christmas bore such joy, while this hilarity seemed so tinny? What a sadness had this panicky laughter, throwing fire so bravely against the night! It was the age-old sound of man terrified by darkness, claiming his gift of fire and hurling it at the spirits of evil. It was the laughter that the Viking heroes must bellow as they died. The sounds of revelry sang to her the words of the Book of Proverbs: "Like fire cackling in a thorn bush is the laughter of a fool."

Yet, there must be good in paying off debts and welcoming your fellows in out of the dark.

A little snow had fallen since Christmas, and during Hogmanay night, mist settled. It froze to every sill and branch and leaf of grass, building in tiny white crystals, white over all, held in the white of mist. The dawning sun breathed the mist away, and in full sun the world was radiant. Margaret had climbed to a small window on the stairs to look out. The country lay clear before her, clear to the farthest hills, soft and brilliant in the sun. All on the land was white crystalline: even stone was glazed with frost. The sky held only a pale blue, and pink blew across it. Every sound fell so purely. A bird sang.

All the sparks of colors refracted from white sang music of frozen things. No warmth or suppleness of life was here, no rich smells of food and nurturing, but neither were the smells and colors of rot. This day God answered Hogmanay with his winter gift. Winter did not give humans sustenance or warmth, but it gave God's beauty in silence. Silence and purity God gave today—a gift like flying in the air.

Margaret stood long at the open window. Finally she ran off to the hall. Who could she find to walk out there with her?

8

Bishop Lanfranc had come from London, staying at Dunfermline a few weeks to learn the news of Scotland. Margaret knelt next to him in the little chapel, after confessing to him as she had many times when they had lived near him.

"Father, will you help me?"

The bishop was leaning his head back against the wall with his eyes closed, as he always did after her confession, listening for the Holy Spirit, and giving his penitent time also to listen.

"Father, I must go. Can you take me with you?"

He lifted his head a little to look at her.

"I'm twenty-three now, Father. Most women would have five children by now. I've made God wait too long, Father. Always there's a reason to wait—a new chance of peace or a new siege. It will never be easy to go.

"From when I was little I've longed to go to the monastery. I've visited many of the holy hermits here in Scotland, wondering if God would like me living here as they do. But Lanfranc—they don't have Mass most days. It's the Mass I'm called to. I've got to have it every day!

"Yes, and the community, too. I couldn't live alone. It's the whole life of a monastery I long for.

"So I've got to leave here. I could go to Ireland or France, or even to Hungary—back to the Sisters who taught me.

"But, Father, not even my mother sees it. Malcolm has it in his head that he must have me for his queen, and my mother thinks he's right. She wants to seal a peace between our two lands; she wants me to carry on the royal family.

"So I must go, and leave no question. For me to stay is hard on us all. Malcolm won't see that there's anyone else he could love until I've gone and made my vows."

"Tell me Margaret," Lanfranc asked, "why do you think the king and your mother are wrong?"

"Why, Father! Father, you know I've given myself to the Lord."

"Get up and sit down, Margaret. Let me ask you to consider a little. What does your mother say?"

"What does my mother say?"

"Yes, what does she tell you?"

"She gives better reasons than Edgar and the others to give up my call. Her reasons are all about the people of Scotland—how they need so much, and how Malcolm needs a queen to help him, and how fit I am to be that person. She talks of how I've been educated, how circumstances have brought me to this very place, how Malcolm himself is naturally drawn to me. She says I have a duty to the people, the duty to help lead them, and that this is a duty to God."

"And what do you tell her?"

"I tell her that such a duty could not override God's troth pledged to me."

"How long have you known this troth, Margaret?"

"From when I began to talk, I knew that our family lived in exile. The king of England with no home to call his own! The people of our land left with no one but whatever brute was strongest to lead them. The more I learned of the commotion, the danger, the fear, the more I wanted to offer *myself* for them.

"And then the beauty and sweetness that the nuns taught us at Mecseknadasda Castle. The gift to read, and to read the Scriptures of God himself! I was shown a way, Father, a way of peace, a way to offer myself that is deeper and stronger than all diplomacy or all force of arms.

"I've come to know our Lord Jesus a little. Father, he has so few friends! I want to be his true friend. I have only myself to give; I want to give at least all of myself to him. I want to wear the white linen of his bride around my face, and the heavy black wool of poverty and penance; to claim nothing but from him! I want to rise each night when the world sleeps and sing his praises! I want to put my hands into the hands of the abbess he gives me and say, 'Do with me what you will!'"

Lanfranc sat long. Margaret kept herself from speaking more.

"So whatever life God has made you for," asked the bishop, "that is what you want? So that his kingdom may come without delay."

"That is what I want," she said.

"Now, look at Malcolm," said the bishop. "See the prospect he has before him. All the people of Scotland depend on him as their father. Clans and clans, to the far directions of all this land. Clans you have not even met.

"Look at the people, living in their little piles of stones, ready to have them knocked over any time one chief takes it into his head that another's offended him.

"Look at the size of their garden plots. Fields? They don't know what a farm field is! What do they have to eat beyond what they can hunt or scrounge from Nature?

"What do they wear? Once it is made, the same thing over and over until it grows into their skins.

"What is it to be born a Scottish infant? The first words you hear as you come from the womb are incantations of fear. If you're as strong as a wild animal and live a few days, you'll hear and feel many more of the works of magic to carry you through the hungry days and the dark days and the days of sickness. You'll grow up learning little more than your mother and your father know—how to grab your survival and fight down whoever might take it away.

"Yes, you'll probably be baptized. And you'll go to the dark, smoky hut they call a kirk, and hear the most beautiful and loving words of Life from God himself. When you're of age, truly you'll receive the King of Heaven bodily. But even in the kirk you'll not learn the whole truth, for your fellow countrymen can't stand the pointy-nosed Romans, and they've made the Mass so Scottish they've lost half the truth.

"When you leave the church, you'll make signs on yourself to ward off evil. You'll spend your life examining birds' entrails and watching the stars and reading omens into all that happens, because the great fear of Dragda and the Three Weird Sisters is the only science you've learned.

"King Malcolm may not see all of this as clearly as you or I, Margaret, but he knows his people need much that he has no inkling how to provide. He loves his people. He'll fight for their freedom, never saving himself. He'll fight for his poor—but if the poor could read, they could defend themselves.

"Malcolm wants to conquer all the evil in Scotland, but he can't even conquer himself. He knows it, Margaret, and when he looks to you, it's more than whim. His people need a mother, Margaret. They need to learn the ways of peace. They need to learn to cultivate food; to be clean; to make things not only to use, but to be beautiful. Yes, they need to see beauty, to make beauty. Often even the beauties of earth and sky and sea they cover with dirt, they hide from in fear; they ruin in order to survive. They are too tired to see.

"You have learned much of the harmony a human being can develop in his life. You know how to study the Scriptures; you can read the philosophers in their own languages. You have me, your friend in London, to help you find those who can educate the Church. You have learned the ways of prayer and order from the Sisters in your uncle's court. Yes, and many crafts and arts of medicine and fine cooking and sewing and managing a great house and farm. More than this, Margaret, you know how to listen to a person and draw out his story. You can hear a people's soul, and where it cries to be led.

"These abilities are not your trophies, Margaret, but God's gifts to give.

"Malcolm is not afraid to lead his people. He gets up each morning to work for them. But he needs to have a home in a woman. He needs someone who will be waiting for him and will run her finger softly down his arm. He needs someone from whom he does not have to cover himself. He needs someone who takes her joy in him. One who lives to provide him his needs, and who longs to see all the good that he will do.

"Margaret, would you not love to be the one to run your finger along his arm?"

Margaret looked down to her hands in her lap for a long time.

"Aye, Father, I would love it too much."

"Are you sure you *can* love it too much, Margaret?"

"Father, it's not usually God's way to count up your talents and worldly preparation. He picked a scroungy, wailing desert tribe to carry his promise. He chose a man with a lisp to lead his people out of Egypt. He took a fisherman to be the Holy Father of all His Church. He chooses *men* to be priests! Talents are nothing to God! He does not need me to help him save Scotland!"

"Aye, Margaret," replied the bishop, "God does not need you to help him save anyone, either in the castle or in the cloister."

Lanfranc sat forward, a little closer to her face.

"Do you know that just when you think you know the ways of God, he flummoxes you? Sometimes he *does* gift and prepare one perfectly for what he would have her do."

"But Christina is as prepared as I!

"And in fact, Father, what Malcolm needs in a woman is that she be Scot! They're buxom, Father, to give him what he needs. First he went for a Norsewoman, and she was too tough for him; now he wants me, who'll never stand up to him. One of his own race would build his native strength to follow the gifts of their blood."

"Margaret, for all your wearing of straight dresses and spending hours in the chapel and making friends with the small and the smelly, you have captured Malcolm's heart. This makes you the most powerful woman in Scotland."

Margaret and the bishop were quiet for a while. Then he spoke again.

"But the call? You say these things are not to be judged according to worldly fitness or personal attraction, but by what God chooses you to do."

"Yes, Father, it's what God tells me in my heart that matters; the reason he made me that I must follow, hoping against hope. He gives me his hand in the darkness of pure faith."

His eyes were half closed, his chin resting on the tips of his joined hands.

"Yes, he speaks in the darkness of faith."

He sat longer.

"So in this darkness you hear God calling you to give yourself to him alone?"

"Yes, Bishop Lanfranc."

"And what does your heart tell you?"

"My heart?"

Margaret was quiet for a while. She gazed on the wide floor stones, following their seams. She raised her gray eyes toward the bishop, but not quite to his eyes.

"Father, my heart pumps with such hot blood that it's hard for me to hear."

"Listen to your heart, Margaret. That is your penance. Ask the Holy Spirit to dwell in your pounding heart, and then listen to your heart, just as it is. You may receive Communion every day this week. Then we'll talk again."

After he had absolved her, Lanfranc stayed praying in the chapel. Then he left her alone.

Two spots of warmth burned on her cheeks, but she was calm with some new warmth of amazement and relief.

Listen to your heart, the bishop had said—he who had so often heard her sins and spoken with her of their longing for God. Lanfranc, who knew the language the world cannot know, who lived to empty himself for Christ. Lanfranc who knew he could do a person no greater kindness than to help her to do the same.

She sat very still. In those days they still did not keep the Blessed Sacrament in church after Mass for people who came to pray, so she turned within herself to the Holy Spirit, whom she knew already dwelt there. She asked him to flood her heart.

So, she said to him in the stillness, *you don't want me to be your bride?*

Some might have expected her to be disappointed. But how could she be? She was no less sure of God's love. In all the tenderness he had shown her, *he* had always known the way he wanted her; she was the one who had not known.

Can it be, Jesus? You want me to listen to my crazy heart? You will be better served if I go after him? In this lifetime you want me to have such exultation? It's the best way I can praise you?

What were these most excited, cool tears?

True, this was only the first day of her seven. She had not yet received Jesus in the Eucharist—seven lovely days ahead. She had not finished listening. But she knew.

I ndeed, it was hard during these next few days for Margaret to keep her reserve. The earth could not hold her down as it had before. She felt she must dance as she walked. She could hardly keep from swinging her skirts. The birds she heard trying their first sweet spring songs seemed to be singing for her, and she wanted to sing with them.

Her hair! She could not but notice its long thickness and think of those herbs she could wash it with that would bring out the shine and lift it lightly with their scent. Surely it wouldn't hurt to start brushing it more!

Her eyes! She *could* not keep them down when she saw Malcolm! When could she share all these wonders with him?

But when the day came to talk again with the bishop, Margaret had drawn herself together strongly.

"Bishop, you must know. When I think of turning my heart to Malcolm, it's not of the people of Scotland I'm thinking. It's not of God's love, and his choice of me for Malcolm and his people. It's of Malcolm I'm thinking."

"I should hope so, Margaret!"

"It's not his immortal soul I'm thinking of either. It's how he is, riding off in the morning with the sun on him. He sits so broad and tall on his horse! They move together, as if they carry the sunbeams. There's nothing that flaps loose on him, Father. He's all alive and together."

She paused.

"It's his silly pride. He loves people to depend on him. He's sure he can save anyone. Even if he's not sure, he doesn't hesitate to protect or to help whomever he sees.—And truly, he does seem to be able to do it. I've never seen him fail—at least in the things of bodily strength and warlike courage. In all the things of the woods, the water, fire, and storms. He has a way with animals. He's clever with his hands, too.

"But how he is with little ones! Ah, I've seen him take one so tiny, and not noble either, and sit him close against his chest in his strong arm, and brush his lips on that soft head of hair. I've seen him take a squalling babe from a tired mother and comfort him against his breast until he sleeps so peacefully the mother can put him to bed.

"He hums. Ah, his humming and his singing! It comes from so deep and it sounds so true—and yet he never knows exactly the tones or the words. His voice is a great man's, and his way is of a boy in school!

"You see, Father? It's ridiculous fancy!

"When he comes into the chapel while I'm there and tries to pray as I do, I should scoff, but it so touches me. I know very well that if I should marry him he would forget about the chapel the next day.

"But here is how I *am*, and not how I *should be*. I've seen him mix water with his ale, as he's seen me do. I *should* recognize that in mimicking a humble act he is merely spreading his peacock's feathers. But I'm quite sure, Father, he cares nothing whether I see him or not. He cares nothing if his *men* see him, and what man is not known by how he holds his ale? Really, he does it because he has seen me do it, and he wants to see what virtue he can find in it that I do."

Lanfranc sat as comfortably as if the bench had a back.

"But no, I still haven't told you. It's how he is putting *me* on a horse—hardly touching me, because of his strength, not his weakness. It's my animal admiration and my longing for the body and the wit of such a man! And have you ever thought, Father, how it is for a woman who should keep her eyes cast down, to be with these Scotsmen who *will* not cover their knees?"

Lanfranc was forty, and his body was lean and smooth-planed, the graying in his hair doing nothing to age him. Funny how God expected him to help with these things of love between man and woman. Indeed, he found it one of his joys. He smiled a little with a sparkle.

"They're grand feelings God gives you, aren't they?"

Still feeling the heat of shame, Margaret kept to her argument.

"Yes, they're grand, Father, but they're blind! My poor body and feelings don't know what my soul wants. The devil pulls them to his pleasure. I don't even need the devil: I have myself! I want so much pleasure, Father, so much love! I could never in this life get all the love—all the pleasure. I've got to chastise myself.

"And I must tell you about how I lie to myself. I want to make Malcolm happy, Father. I want to lift the dark sadness from his eyes and show him the ways I know. I think I can listen to him as no one can. I even hope to show him how close he is to his dear Jesus.

"See how vain I am? He'll stay about as he is, and when God wants to show himself to him, God will do it with or without me. And can I bear the faults he has? For right now, I hardly believe he has any."

The bishop answered, "You know you're besotted. Knowing, you're ahead. And if you're somewhat senseless, it comes from God. Let us talk of serious things, even though now you may not feel them. You can still store them in your mind.

"Don't worry, dear lady, your self will be knocked to the ground many a time. You are right: in this life you *will* never get enough pleasure, or enough love. That's one reason God gives these grand feelings—to get you into all the trouble you are about to get into! And to carry you through it.

"Another reason, truly, is that God couldn't stand to take everything after Adam and Eve let it go. He had designed such beautiful delights for us, and he was so disappointed. He couldn't put us so far out of paradise for so long!

"Even aside from being the queen of Scotland, you will know, many a day, such loneliness and such despair of ever doing good. You will feel your trust betrayed. If not betrayed, you will at least feel disappointed. God told woman in the very beginning—in the third chapter of Genesis: 'Your yearning shall be for your husband, yet he will lord it over you.' Watch. No matter how good a man Malcolm is, no matter how much he loves you, he cannot help it; he will lord it over you. And you: ah, you shall yearn for him!

"You will not have to ask Jesus to let you share his sorrow, Margaret. You will know the tiredness he felt often as he set out to preach; you will know others' irritation that you will not let them be as they are—yes, and their misunderstanding. In all of your life with Malcolm you will know the hardship Jesus felt in his home town, in his public life, and you will know his abandonment in Gethsemane.

"You worry you'll take your love of God and give it to Malcolm? God may not let you vow yourself all to him on the first day, but vow yourself to Malcolm in God's arms without fear, and you will be able to pour all your life out for God.

"You may not put on the poor white and black each day, but you'll need more joy and love to drape yourself always in rich colors, and keep your hair shining and bejeweled; to smell clean and fragrant for your husband and your people. You may not rise each night with the Matins bell to praise God, but many a night you'll be able to praise him as you nurse your babies, as you sit by the sick, as you lie listening, comforting your husband in all his anxieties.

"Every Scots child God gives you when you put your hand into Malcolm's is Christ. Can you get enough of prayer with God, my lady, when from the time you rise, each child you hold, each person you serve, each one you instruct, is Christ putting himself in your arms? Yes, and from before you rise—all the night long. For even if there were not Scotland, not one child counting on you, but only Malcolm—you would have the one God dedicates to you.

"What is the best gift, the greatest strength you can give your Malcolm?

"Delight in him! Do not hold yourself back! A man knows if his wife is free with him. He knows if it's real, and there is no sweetness like it.

"Savor each tender piece of meat he puts in your mouth, Margaret. *Forget yourself* in delight. Don't worry, he will feed you plenty of bites of gristle, too. Then, too, you can forget yourself."

Margaret was very quiet. She was glad that Lanfranc never seemed to count time when they talked of things of the Spirit. She looked past his face, at the window carved into the dark stone wall. The glass was not clear enough for her to see the things happening outside, but across it was the movement of the clouds in the spring wind constantly changing the light.

"So, Father," she said, at last looking into his brown eyes, "you are telling me to change very much the way I am living? Where I have been keeping myself contained, you are saying, 'Open!' What I have tried to shun, you say, 'Embrace!' The rules and guides and structures I have kept for support, you say, 'Let go! You will not fall. God will give you his support. He will lead you closely in the same poverty you have desired, in a *greater* poverty.'"

"Yes, Margaret. God has trained your soul to this point. Do not be afraid! Your Lord will show you everything each day in your Communion. And if he comes to you in your husband or your family some days and takes you from Communion, he will make sure that he comes even closer to you in them."

"I do know, Father, that if Malcolm will have me I will not escape to ease. I *should* be terrified. I had thought I would have the sure bounds of a monastery, so that I could reach deep within. But now I must reach out to the borders of Scotland. Not only to Scotland: I must search the world to find its best. I must learn the language and the pleasure of world leaders; give them such hospitality that we can work peace. I must bring the poor together with the haughty; seek the gifts of the great that will feed us. We will always be at war—if not with force of arms, then against black magic, and most of all, against ignorance and gossip. Even at war with the vermin!

"Now I will never offer up a louse bite as a sacrifice! Now it will not be for myself but for Malcolm that I'll chase them down! He'll not have a louse in his bed!"

"You can write me, too, Margaret. I will send you a priest named Turgot. All of us priests, even if we ourselves can't help you, we can give you Jesus in the Sacraments.

"You'll find advisors, too. And I think your Malcolm will make you strong, whether he understands you or not."

"But at this moment I am not at all afraid, Lanfranc. That God would *want* me to seek for Malcolm's arms! To have him, to hold him, to be his, to forget myself in him, you say! That God would give me this! How could he deny me anything I need that comes with Mael Colum?"

The bishop smiled. She was amazed at how simply he, this handsome, warm man of forty, and she, whom she knew was very beautiful to men, could be talking so simply of such usually secret things.

"Then you are not having a hard time seeing how free you must be? You tend toward mortification, Margaret. You do not choke on this new way of mortification? To accept all joy and pleasure as freely as you accept disappointment, loneliness and duty? That your only penitential exercise will be to *pursue* good? 'Seek good and pursue it,' the psalmist says. *Run after it.*

"So you do begin to understand, Margaret, that if Malcolm takes you as his wife, you can do nothing better than to *delight* in him? You cannot love Malcolm too much. Give yourself so freely to him, even though it seems dreamy. All the love and truth of God will come with it.

"Think often of what St. Paul tells us, that the union of husband and wife is an image of the union of God with his people. The psalmist says, 'Take delight in the Lord and he will grant you your heart's desire.' So you take delight in your espoused lord. And since he is not God, many times he will not grant you your heart's desire. Then you will be getting your desire to begin to know what Jesus felt in his agony. Yes, before you are finished, you will know his immolation."

They had talked long enough. They sat silently together. Then she knelt for absolution.

"Stay. Spend as much time as you have with Jesus in the church," he said. "Don't underestimate the Virgin Mary. Ask her! You will be amazed at the faerie dust she loves to sprinkle on the marriage bed!"

Once Margaret was alone in the church, her tears gave way. How could they keep coming so? After some time, a light silence, like fresh spring, carried her soul.

But this time her prayer did not stretch on into dalliance. She had things to do. What if Malcolm had lost interest?

10

ow were the days like a long and vigorous country dance, Margaret escorted by the truest prince of the land. For there had been little to accomplish between Margaret and Malcolm. Frightening it was how much could gestate under so much restraint! Through all the days and nights, Margaret carried in her heart this sweet closeness to Malcolm, the assurance that they would soon be one.

But in the meantime, all those people they were taking on by their union pulled their sleeves and turned their ears. The clans sent news only of rejoicing that their Chief-of-Chiefs was taking Margaret as his queen. Why these Scots did not hold this Saxon-blooded refugee in more contempt, Margaret could not tell. Those around her said that it was because she had already been so good to them. Perhaps they were glad enough just that their throne would now be balanced by a woman. Maybe they simply looked forward to the great pageant and feast that their king would provide. And if there was jealousy, it would likely come out in unsuspected treachery.

But what came to their doors each day were gifts upon gifts—lines of people both prosperous and poor, with their best lamb, or a fine weaving, or metalwork or leatherwork, or good ale, or their fierce distilled drink. People came with offers to play the pipes or to lead a dance, or to help with all that must be done.

Agatha seemed created for this moment. This wedding must be a memorable feast for all of Scotland, she said, and that was Margaret and Malcolm's duty. They belonged to their people and must forget any personal inclinations toward understatement. They owed it to their people to accept graciously all their gifts and to give in return a celebration of such beauty and plenty as to renew their pride, and their hope in all things good. Margaret knew this was true. She went along lightly with the different plans that kept coming, colliding, and branching out more.

She was somewhat vexed that her mother had presumed so much as to import all manner of wedding finery from the Continent, and carry it with them on their very flight to Dunfermline! But all these could as well have been for Christina, or, indeed, for any Gaelic queen. And her mother's practicality meant that with no wait they could prepare as lavish a feast as might satisfy the courts on the continent.

There were gold and silver goblets, dishes, and candlesticks. There were gorgeous hangings for behind the place of coronation and for behind the head table. There was a damask table cloth. There was a fine, heavy ring she could give to Malcolm, needing only to be engraved. There was one, too, that might be suitable for her, but Margaret would not have it. If Malcolm gave her a ring, it would be his ring, fashioned as he desired.

There were some little trifles and sweetmeats, too: enough for small favors for a great number of guests.

There was silk for her wedding shift, and silk, too, for the first wife's wimple that Malcolm would put on her head. An array of fine fabrics there was, and delicate jewelry, too, to augment the bride's trousseau. There were even dresses sewn to her size! Margaret bit her lip only a little to keep her grace and show whole-hearted thanks.

For the altar of the wedding Mass there were fine white cloths, and also some of the Opus Anglicum, richly embroidered in gold, both for altar and priest's vestments. There were brilliant, pounded-gold altar vessels, the chalice and paten set with jewels.

More than her mother, Margaret was watchful that these foreign imports be not shown too much esteem. She traveled the country round to be advised by the wise and the skillful in the ancient traditions. For many of the cloths and trappings of the wedding she chose carefully from the best of all that the Scots themselves made. The food and drink served must be of their land. Yes, a little French wine, too. And every gift brought to their door would be used on their wedding day for that feast for which it was intended.

Margaret and Malcolm prepared their souls, too, for the Sacrament God had made to reflect for the world his marriage with his people. Malcolm did think it mostly nonsense, sitting with the pale Turgot and cutting capers with one's mind about something so simple. And, indeed, it was much easier to kiss bishops' rings, grant land to monasteries, and carry the cross in processions, than it was to seek out one's sins and confess them kneeling. But he knew great joy with his absolution, and all things that Margaret revered, he wanted greatly to value.

Margaret's brother Edgar knew well how to stale joy with small, jealous pokes and prods, and there were enough other snubbed egos and strong opinions to make peacefulness a constant work of art. But Malcolm was indulgent, being very pleased at this beautiful match and this significant event for Scottish pride. So, by the night before, Margaret found that she slept well, at least half the night, and when she looked into the polished metal mirror in the morning, found no circles under eyes.

11

The window was small in the gray stone chapel, but the beams coming through it seemed to carry all the bright sunlight that filled the green land outside. Their light gleamed on the white altar cloth, casting a soft blue shadow of the cross. It danced lightly with the two white-gold candle flames and fluttered in the creamy flowers of Easter. The gifts to be offered on the altar waited on a smaller table—pure wheaten bannocks and deep red wine. Bishop Fathad had closed the great, jeweled Book of the Gospel and asked them to come stand with him. To Margaret, all things seemed twice real.

Margaret stood before Malcolm, tall but gentle in her soft, blue wool dress. Her hair glinted red and gold in heavy twists held by thin, brilliant blue ribbons twined with white hyacinth flowers. The ribbons showed her eyes cornflower blue, those eyes that for the first time looked in Malcolm's full openly. Malcolm smelled of the clean oat fields and of sun-dried wool. He was without clanking metal and hard leather, for he wore not a weapon. He had only a wide leather belt, and a shoulder brooch held his plaid. His face, too, was quiet, though the quiet in his dark eyes was of smoldering fire.

She heard his words in Latin, as she had asked him to say them, and she answered the same in Latin. Then she heard the words in Gaelic, and she answered him in the same light, Gaelic sounds that made his eyes burn so fiercely.

Yes, Mael Colum, before God, until death shall pull us apart!

The bishop took their gifts—their gifts and those of all the people.

Take us, Father. Let your Son make us an everlasting gift to you.

When they came from the chapel after the marriage Mass, the court of Dunfermline Abbey was pulsing with the crowd. Many more, too, they said, were pushing from outside, where, indeed, more long trestle tables had been set up to ensure welcome for all. Margaret, Malcolm, and Bishop Fathad ascended some steps that stood high to reach the formal doorway, high enough that many outside the abbey wall could see them. There the bishop blessed her as Queen, and placed the crown on her head, heavy and unyielding. The robe, heavy, too, though soft, was clasped around her shoulders with the gleaming queenly brooch. She was now Mother of them all!

Graciously she greeted her people, and they cried out their loyalty. She took Malcolm's hand—he, too, now heavily crowned and robed—and together they came down the steps to their Scots. For many hours afterward she walked among them, sometimes with Malcolm, sometimes by herself, to receive the kiss of one after another; to ask about this one and that; to hold a child; to see that all were drinking and eating as they wished.

She and Malcolm had their hours, too, of presiding at the head table, being served all the courses proper to such a feast. It came time for Malcolm to toast her. How carefully his seneschal poured the fine wine, taking his little tasting cup so solemnly. He filled Malcolm's heavy gold goblet near to the top, and Malcolm took it and turned to her, holding it steadily. She felt his hand softly on her back as he lifted the cup to her lips and tilted it just enough for her to sip. How well she knew this ceremony, how practiced she was for her part. Yet, for all the crowd and the concerns of the feast, his touch, his careful giving her to drink, his eyes so close and not looking away, were all she knew. How was it she took her turn offering him the cup without spilling a drop, as her whole body trembled as though not her own?

Then came the other toasts, and all were kind and full of welcome. Margaret, and Malcolm, too, hardly dared accept that joy and welcome should be so universal. The day, the whole day, was sunshine and blessing from God, and in all she did, Margaret was singing him thanks.

There were skits and performances, dancing and drinking, and the pipes. For all the rest of her life, whenever Margaret heard the pipes—for such joyous days as this; when whining the terrible call to war; when announcing a pale, still body being brought home on a pallet—Margaret would always think of those glorious, heavenly skirlings of their marriage day. She would pray for the day when the only sounds the pipes would play would be the sounds of the Wedding Feast.

Before folk had begun to stagger and taunt, the time came for the wedding couple to be escorted to their bower. For this night, the bridal bed was made up in a loft room outside the great hall. After the feasting it would be moved to the large cupboard of King and Queen in the hall.

The sheepskins were spread with linen sheets, bleached dry on the sweet grass under the sun. There were two large goose down pillows, cased in linen. Strewn all over the bed were the herbs and flowers of the field. Above the bed hung a silver cross.

Margaret's mother lit the candle, though the soft blue light of dusk still filled the room, and blessed them. When she closed the door, the sounds of feasting left them to themselves. The soft song of a chickadee came in on the evening air. Everything seemed twice real.

12

The days after everyone had left the wedding feast were days like the happy songs of the troubadours. Mael Colum was like a youth. He was so overjoyed to have such a bride, he would have nothing but her music. He would wake her in the night and he would wake her at first dawn, just because he could. He came to Mass with her, and though he tried to respect her morning hours of prayer, sometimes he could not wait for whatever plans he had for them. Then those plans became her prayer. At any time, he might come in with a brace of dripping birds for her, or a vast bunch of flowers from the field.

If his duties of state were not pressing, he liked to take her "a-viking," as he said, to the places he had wanted to show her since she came. He would take her to new villages and families, and show her the best flour mill or the surest salmon pool. He had her review his army at Dunfermline and then the one at Edinburgh. They rode along the borders and conversed with the sentries. And always he looked for hermits and for holy shrines, thinking that these must be her dearest interest.

Sometimes in the middle of day he would snatch her hand and tell her to get her riding dress quickly. They would leave with no word to anyone but the grooms who sent them off. He would have a lunch strapped to his saddle, and they would take off on their horses down back paths and on trails through pines, often letting their horses have their heads. How was it that he so soon had them in some place with no soul in sight? If anyone did watch them, that person knew he was impertinent! Most folk did not suspect they were gone before they were back. No bodyguard! Malcolm's men knew well not to follow unless called. Here he was most like a man of twenty—never a thought but that *his* protection was all that any woman might need.

He would stop at the top of a boiling falls and pick her up like a child, holding her out over the edge.

"See, I'll not drop you!"

And, really, she felt small fear. What could be so bad about crashing on the rocks of a Scottish spate while together so close?

Other days they would sneak out a back castle door and straight into the fields. They knew how to move fast until they got to grass tall enough for them to make themselves a place where they could be seen by no one. Malcolm would put down a piece of hide to protect Margaret from the dew, and they would sit talking and listening, free, with only heaven knowing.

The longer they sat there, the more the creatures who lived among the grasses would show themselves, picking up the tasks they could not hold up forever just in honor of a visiting king and queen. The insects had no patience whatever—the grasshoppers, the ants, the bees, the lady bugs and beetles. They kept hopping and humming and scurrying and crawling even as Malcolm and Margaret first parted the grass. The spiders held still at first, but soon went on with their webs or their travels. Then the birds would start back to singing. Once, Margaret and Malcolm had stayed still long enough that a quail mother returned to her nest, which they had not seen so close to them. A groundhog would rise out of its hole and stand stock-still, seeming not even to move its eyes, until finally it would drop a little, then move a little more, then slip away—and perhaps return later. The garter snakes would again take up their trails so rudely blocked by two hulking humans. If they were by a burn, there were the muskrats, the frogs and salamanders, the water skippers, dragonflies; and gnats and the small trout that came for them. All of this, to watch and listen to, was enough that they were never ready to leave.

One brilliant day, Malcolm lay with his head on a tussock of grass and his feet in the creek. The bobbing grass heads cast their shadows across his face. Margaret rested against his arm.

She said,

"Mael Colum, how does it feel to kill someone?"

His face caught a little, and his smile was rueful.

"You think of strange things while sitting in the grasses and the flowers!"

"They say you killed MacBeth. And Lulach, too. You must have killed many to keep Scotland free."

"Margaret, you don't think of how you feel when you kill a man. You can't, or you'd never do what has to be done. Why do you think we paint ourselves with blue and ochre, and screech like demons, going to battle? We're making ourselves *not* ourselves. We leave our selves behind. One possessed does the killing."

Very quietly and slowly, she said,

"What do you feel like when you slash a man? When you see a brother of yours, built by God and only a moment ago working so beautifully—brain, muscles, sinews, heart—see him as a heap of meat—nothing there but food for maggots? When you know he's someone's husband, someone's father, someone's son? That God has protected him, urged him, tickled him all these years to such health and ability, and you have finished him in a moment?"

"Margaret," he answered, "you do not think those things when you kill a man. You think of what he has done to your father, of what his father did to your father, and of what he will do to all whom you love, if you do not stop him. You think of the group he's one of, and of all your people who must die, be raped, be burned out—who will never have peace if those men triumph. You don't think of killing, Margaret, you think of saving from death."

Margaret stayed still, listening.

"No," he continued, "you never think of what you did, if you can. After it is done, you hug your fellow defenders. You wash yourself hard in the cold stream. You bring home your fallen with music and tears, and bury them with honor. And you give generously to widows and orphans of your dead. You give to every child and woman and man as much as you can. And, oh, how happily you hold close any sweet, innocent child! When you come back from war, how dearly you love your wife to take you in her arms with all tenderness!"

Still Margaret sat quietly.

"Aye, Margaret, I am covered in blood. I still cannot believe God could give you to me—a woman of such pure peace—innocent, innocent before every human being on the earth! I cannot know how you could say Yes.

"I never thought you would, Margaret. I swaggered so surely, but I was no more myself then than I am when I kill a man. I knew I'd sooner or later be finding someone else.

"Do you know that I was terrified our first night? Indeed I'd prayed nine days in a row that you would not die when I took you.

"Do you know that I, too, went for counsel to the priest? I could not have had the courage to take you if he'd not convinced me it was God's will."

Margaret chuckled lightly.

"You think I am pure peace, do you? You don't know all the murder I've done in my thoughts. And then, maybe only because I do not like the way someone makes me sew with gold thread.

"Aye, Mael Colum, you're a good man, and I don't think you've ever done evil on purpose. I cannot see how you men do the things you do. Most of all, what you great leaders must do, who turn the tide for whole clans of people. Before heaven, I cannot see how it's right! But I am small, and I eat white pudding. I have never saved one person from danger. I'd not be so sweetly sitting in this grass if you had not done what you've done. No one would in this land. All of us would be thralls.

"Think that we have been able to talk of this, Mael Colum! I often think on it, but I need the field creatures with me to ask you!"

13

The fire burned low in the quiet hall as Malcolm and Edgar sat yet at the table. Malcolm was alive with conviction. He urged Edgar point by point. Edgar's intensity was of the strained kind which gave Margaret such foreboding.

Often had these two talked thus. Only a few days after he had taken the family in to Dunfermline, Malcolm had offered Edgar his strong arm.

"It's a crime what they've done to you! How can I let it rest? We'll go back, Edgar! I'll be by your side, and my army with yours. We'll have them before the year's over, my good friend, and you'll lead your own people."

Edgar had hardly been able to answer then. He withdrew in a way so strange to Malcolm! What could Malcolm do but retreat, too, in deference? He had broached his offer. Let Edgar know that he was ready to discuss these matters when Edgar was ripe for it.

But never did Edgar return to the subject until Malcolm would raise it again, when they had more news of the Normans' aggression. The hall would rock with hot talk that night, and then when folk began to retire, Malcolm would hold Edgar back and make him sit to talk earnestly. Edgar would entertain his proposals, but never did he have his own concerns or plans to put forth.

Already, Malcolm was saying tonight, they could have had allies lined up well down into the English country, ready to greet them and join forces if they but rode there. Who in the country loved the Normans? They awaited only a leader.

But so much time had slipped by without Edgar sending out any communications. Now, at least, they had heard from an earl in North Umbria looking for them to come; offering all the forces he commanded.

"This is our start!" Malcolm swore. "We haven't been able to feel the lay of the land from up here. Now we know a friend. If he's writing to us, he's writing to others. He knows what he can count on. We'll go, Edgar! We can't plan a vast operation from here. We take our army, we join their army, and we pick up another and another day by day and move forward."

Edgar's face was pinched with duty. He agreed falteringly, tentatively. He agreed enough to sound an earnest rightful king and go to bed in peace.

"How long can you let this droning Frenchman enthrall your people?" Malcolm demanded, rising from the table in frustration. "Your own flesh and blood are mucking out their stalls, emptying their bathtubs and chamber pots, bending their faces to the Normans' feet! The children of Edmund Ironside and good King Edward have lost their lands! Can any of them go to school or run a trade? Do any of them open their mouths in a court? Whose bonds of matrimony are safe? Your people, grown from Angles' Land, and they are nothing in the land but serfs to usurpers.

"How can you stand it, Edgar? What is this 'right time' you wait for? If I were you, I'd be after them now. I'd be glad at least to die for what's rightful, rather than sit twisting my belly over whether or not I could win!

"He's *French*, Edgar. French! He eats soufflés and truffles! He sings to ladies and wears perfume!"

This was the night when Edgar finally committed. In the next days Margaret watched with a sinking heart as they prepared to march. She knew this must happen. How many of her people waited for them to act? What language would William hear but the clash of the sword?

Edgar—Margaret prayed to believe in him. She prayed that a self hidden in him would blossom. But she felt as much as she felt her own life: It was not in him. He would ride with his army, he would parlay, he would strive to incite his men, but he would be no more than an actor in the part. Strong leaders could give him their hand. They could pull him along. When they let go, he would stand there, an empty suit of armor.

Already she imagined with dread the sorties they would make. Malcolm would see their opportunities, engineer a fine attack, urge Edgar on as they rallied ardent troops, swelling as they marched to war. How many men would fall, and if the battle was even won, how long would it take Edgar to lose his ground?

But let time pass, and how could they not make another effort, knowing the straits Edgar's people were in, his duty to them, and Malcolm's loyalty to Edward Confessor's line?

Could she be hoping that her own brother would meet death and settle it all? God forgive her! Never worry. Edgar would not die in battle. He was the kind who never did.

None too soon had they decided to go, either. For before all was even ready, an envoy arrived from William, demanding that Malcolm send Edgar immediately back to the Conqueror. Such arrogance sizzled in the terse, official phrases which the messenger read! Malcolm's harboring the Atheling family had enraged William enough; his taking Margaret as his wife had almost driven William out of his head.

Indeed, it tickled Malcolm.

"Do you know, Margaret, I almost could have married you without loving you just for this lovely effect! Why should God like me so? With one stroke he sends me the angel of my life and sends the Bastard an adder to bite his fat heart!"

They left one morning early, and Margaret bid them farewell, sick for the fathers of families who would lose their lives or be ruined on this venture; for wives and children now dwelling in their quiet homes who would be burned up in fire and violence. She watched them down the road, and felt for the first time the full weight of care for Dunfermline and the whole Scots land. Here she stood, outside the castle, a few youths and old men to guard them, and all the homes on the land, stretching out far beyond what she could see, resting their peace on this house. How long would she be queen alone? Think not of whether Malcolm would return. Christ must be her staff!

And, indeed, she leaned heavily on him as she went back in the castle gate.

14

Most tender pledge between the king and his wife as he left for North Umbria was the child Margaret carried under her heart. It was good that by then she had established a regular way of life for Dunfermline. Her mother had laid the way, and she and Christina were often by Margaret's side. Having worked with those who held offices in the household, Margaret had been able naturally to introduce her ways, and to assign people to the tasks she believed they could best do. Bartholomew had proved himself so adaptable that Malcolm had sent him to govern Edinburgh Castle. Margaret could count on her own mormaer to work openly with her, overseeing castle and lands at Dunfermline. Already she had women close to her who were training in needlework and fine household crafts. She and the cook were on good terms, and it was the same with those who cleaned the house, those who managed the clothes; with the stable staff and with the military. Closest to her was the almoner, whose care was the poor. Now, with an arrangement of life in the house and many to help her, it was not so difficult to get through the times when she felt so sick.

When does a woman long to be with familiar people and familiar ways more than when she is expecting a child? Margaret had never known long, uninterrupted years to make certain customs her own. Did this lighten the longing or make it more urgent? How glad she was to have her family with her, especially her mother! But she knew she could not cling to them. She could not help feeling so adrift as she went to the Scots midwives with her physical problems, and prepared her mind to let these so foreign women help her to give birth.

Then Edward came. The little one had waited for his father to return! Margaret had thought she would die, but she did not, and then she was holding him in her arms, she again in the arms of Malcolm. Such a soft, smooth, round little head, tinged with the copper of both father's and mother's hair! His face was still folded together, but each wrinkle in the lips, each fine hair of the eyebrows, was a marvel. His hands, now clenching, now groping, had in them the power someday to swing an axe or to forge iron. His voice, now sweet like a girl's and trembling, carried in it the power someday to put courage into the hearts of great crowds of men.

The Scots midwives had not let her down. They knew their way in these things of birth and new mothering, and they were kind and gentle, for all their rough manners. That she had given herself over to them to hold her life and the life of her son was as great a triumph as the birth itself. Was her fear of them a little less? Was friendship hidden there?

The Scotswomen did not take it amiss that Margaret kept her child to suckle him.

"I have milk," Margaret said, "and it came for Edward. As long as I can, I'll give him his own mother's strength."

The wives agreed. How could there be soul in such royalty and fine people as bound their own breasts and passed their children to strangers, as though milk were not like blood?

But *Edward* they named him? Not even a gesture toward the House of Dunchada, nor to the line of more than thirty Scottish kings gone before him? Malcolm did have his first three sons: Duncan, named for his father; Domnall, for his brother; and little Malcolm for himself. Was it no more than right that his wife should give this son the name of her sacrificed father? Edward was a new name in Scotland, to be sure!

The three older brothers could not hold and play with their new brother enough. Now did they come out of themselves, so ingenious in their games with him, so tender to make him happy. Enough times they forgot themselves with him that they forgot themselves with Margaret, too.

With these three brothers, with all the children who came in to play, and with all in the house who wanted to hold and care for him, Margaret hardly had a chance to hold her own son. But in the night he was hers. Malcolm loved the tiny baby to sleep with them, often himself taking him in his arms when the child did not need to nurse. Used as he was to sleeping in war camp with a hand on his sword, he feared not to roll over on his son. Indeed, he slept with him so lightly cradled in his arm while Margaret stretched out and rested deep.

When they were together in their curtained-off closet, Margaret perhaps doing some handwork as they talked, Malcolm would take little Edward and lie with him on his chest. The boy could soon hold up his head, and he would brace himself on his small elbows and gaze gravely into his father's eyes. Malcolm would gaze back, and would tell him all the great things of the world. Edward would tell his father the secrets he knew from the womb. Quietly they spoke to each other, Edward holding his head so high and strong, the new, dark blue eyes never leaving the brown-flecked eyes under the weathered brows. Never in their lives would the father and son speak to each other as straightforwardly as they did now.

15

thelrede was the next child to come, and then Edgar, Edmund, Edith (later changed to Matilda), Alexander (named for Pope Alexander), David, and Mary. Through all that might happen in the kingdom, the children were born. Through pressures from kings and chiefs, through civil tensions, through building and entertaining and innovating, through disasters and wars and gossip, and through peace, sometimes with Malcolm near Margaret and sometimes while she guarded his throne, year by year their children came. Margaret found she was strong to carry them and strong to give them birth.

With each child was the memory of the happenings that had accompanied his birth, whether they were peaceful or fraught with worry. There were stories to tell for laughter. Always the child came as a blessing and a light. If his parents were strained to care for him well, his brothers and sisters, the servants and court, and Margaret's friends the poor gave him all he needed.

That she lost none in birth, too, Margaret knew she owed to her Scots midwives. These times when life hung in the balance, she and the wives could get angry with one another. Agatha, in her worry, might speak harsh words. But Margaret let her nurses direct her. Were they helping her or were they not? Thus submitting, she won their respect and love. Always, words of congratulation were tumbled in with words asking forgiveness.

In handing herself over to her adopted people, Margaret forged a bond with them. Through Edward's birth, and then Ethelrede's, and then with Edgar and the others, the more she cast her care on her people, the less she compared them with what else might be.

It did not always go as well as it had at Edward's birth. Margaret had to overcome horror and desolation when she or her children were hurt. They lost Ethelrede when he was young, and Malcolm's young son Malcolm, too. By instinct she tended to doubt those who helped her, but by reason and prayer she reconciled herself to human limitations. Catching her Blessed Mother's hand, she learned her way of gratitude. In depending upon these people of hers, in working with them, and in the joy of triumphs, Margaret gradually came to feel that she belonged to her people, and they to her.

Now, with a growing family, Margaret and Mael Colum may not have darted out into a field often on whimsy, but the flames first lit burned deep and hot. In each new child they saw each other anew, and God within them. And the troubadour's song never left their life. Malcolm would often sit gazing at something Margaret loved—a piece of artwork or a holy book—reverently, as if it spoke her secret. Romance drove him more than once to have a book bejeweled and most gorgeously worked in gold or beautifully enshrined, as a token to her of his heart. Never did Margaret raise an eyebrow at how his extravagance might better have served the poor. What they did for each other was theirs alone.

There was almost nothing that Margaret did which the king did not try. That this exquisite woman of his valued anything made it fascinating to him. They came together to serve dinner to the poor, and to treat those who were sick. He found himself paying the ransom of one English slave and then another, against all reason. When Margaret had almost lost courage to ask him for another costly project, he surprised her as he gave way so easily. Nor did he resent that she approached many beyond himself for the things she felt God asked. Malcolm did find himself much better at serving and tending sores than he was at kneeling still in long prayer. And he did not try to read those books of hers he loved to hold. The Anglo-Saxon Chronicle tells us that "her customs pleased him and he thanked God who had by his power given him such a consort." Malcolm would put himself to almost anything if he knew she desired it. He even fulfilled her greatest desire, that he desire God.

Those who wrote of Malcolm and Margaret during their time tell us little about their life with their children. The family life, that life which was most important to them, remains intimate with them. The personality of each child, the events around their births and development, the hardships and illnesses, the two parents' struggles to agree—these stay within the family as they lived then. We do know that Margaret took each of her children on her lap to teach him, and that she continued as their first educator. It was customary in those times for noble children to be handed to a nurse from birth, to be assigned a staff to raise and educate them, and to be sent as adolescents to learn in another court, or in a monastery school. Without many material amenities and with the duties of lord and lady to their vassals, gentle parents might have only the time with their children which was set aside formally each day. These children of Canmore did go to other houses as adolescents, but until then Margaret kept them by her, and it was she who taught them the things of God.

Edward, Ethelrede, Edgar, Edmund, Edith, Alexander, David, Mary. Five resounding Saxon names, and three from the Church. What of the debt to Scottish ancestry? Did this not warm the talk? High could the blood of the chieftains rise, especially the farther away they were. And high could the talk rise, fueled with ale!

"Aye, the wolf shall lie down with the lamb, alright, and beg for her every instruction!"

"Who is it, anyway, that slipped it over on us to become a flock of bleating boney-heads? Who bewitched us to make lions want to chew the cud? Was it the holy Columkille and his meek Christ? No, for he taught us *Christus vincit.* Nay, it's Margaret who's bewitched the king. And she'll have us all!"

And yet, when she met you, she disarmed you. If she came to your village or you came to her hall, when you met her you knew she could not despise you. You knew you were the one she had been waiting for. You had not suspected your intelligence or your gifts until she showed them to you. You were not embarrassed to make little sallies that might look inept. You tried them proudly, for she saw their greatness.

If you'd not met her, then you talked with one who worked with her: Her servants. Her poor. Her nurses. This woman Margaret did not look past you. She did not have a scheme. She loved you. She wanted to give you all the good she knew.

But when she was not there with you, there was good kindling for resentment. More than *Edward, Ethelrede, Edgar, Edmund* and *Edith.* This Saxon queen of Malcolm's was openly establishing Saxon and European over Scottish! She saw not how she could be a good queen to them unless she did.

Queen Margaret argued that it was Christ she wanted to set free among them. She could show you, too, from the Scriptures and from the Church Fathers, and with her clear mind, how this was so. When she said it of the Church, it was hard to deny. But of other customs—a good wife had spoken the heart of it:

"You, know, Kenneth, that the good queen wants only Christ for us. That she does. You see her, you meet her, you hear her words— you cannot but know she does. But who gave her Christ? The

Saxons. The king of Hungary. The royal courts. The monasteries. Christ can come a thousand ways, but to her, he came through them. What man of us can tell the gift itself from the way he got it? You know yourself, Kenneth. Would not all the world be a happy place if we but ate your mother's cooking?"

So, though villages grew brighter, and people learned more widely, and more men and women were free; though generations grew who did not see war; though beauty and festivity developed for all to behold, still Donald Bane found many a chief who was glad to put his head close and speak of restoring the true Scots spirit.

16

The stone stood about two feet high, in the middle of a wide space of mossy rock, a short walk from the castle. Every day, during the time in the afternoon when children nap, Margaret came and sat on the stone. Any who wished to speak with her came to her there. She had a few guardsmen with her, as Malcolm required, but they took their places well back from her, so that she and her visitors could converse out of their hearing.

From her first months as queen, Margaret had sought such a stone. It was one thing to take people's hands in a large gathering and exchange warm wishes, but quite another to hear seriously what any shy person might have on his heart. Now she had found a place to sit where any person in the realm could come to her without knocking at a gate, answering to a sentry, or explaining to a chamberlain. All could see for themselves how their queen was occupied, and know the reason for their wait. They would see her, though she was queenly attired, sitting without even a backrest to protect her from them, or to give her more rest than they.

Some days no one would be on the little rise when Margaret came to sit. Some days she might sit for the whole time reading a book. Other days, people stood in lines, and some had to go home without speaking with her. But they knew she would be there the next day.

It was matters of judgment which had first prompted Margaret to begin her custom. She wanted people to have recourse if they did not think they had received justice in an official court. As folk came to count on Queen Margaret's Stone, they began to ask her counsel there on less urgent matters, to tell her their good news, or only to confer with her a little because they wanted to know her.

When people came with physical needs, Margaret might take off something she was wearing and give it to them. Or she would turn to one of the guard and ask *him* for his cloak or his shoes. Indeed, it was the joke that anyone accompanying Queen Margaret should never wear or carry something he did not want to lose. That was not easy, for Margaret demanded that her attendants dress well for their courtly services. Who owned more than one or two of the kind of apparel fitting to accompany a queen? Even so, anyone who gave up a possession to her sooner or later received back from her something finer than he had given.

But more often than she handed a supplicant some material gift, she drew the person up strictly. She believed highly of each person, and could not stand self-abasement. As Father Turgot, her chaplain at the castle, wrote of her:

> For the queen united so much strictness with her
> sweetness of temper, so great pleasantness with her
> severity, that all who waited upon her, men as well
> as women, loved her while they feared her, and in
> fearing loved her. Thus it came to pass that when
> she was present, no one ventured to utter even one
> unseemly word, much less to do aught that was
> objectionable.

A beggar might come with a story of being victimized and fully ill-treated, but the story dissolved in his mouth when he looked into her face, so honest, so reverent of him. A fishwife might come to her hot with the rage of gossip, but end by asking if she could come to learn a craft that was being taught in the king's hall.

Margaret was not on her stone to pacify or gratify. All the time that she sat there, she was praying. She asked each person to tell his story fully. She enjoyed the person, sympathized with him, learned from him, and asked his help. She called on him to do what he owed to God and to his brothers and sisters. Many a time she sent a person away with a reproof, or with a challenge to heal a wound, to gain some new skill, or to begin an enterprise, and to report to her as their work progressed.

Queen Margaret's Stone so gently became a custom that few asked the amazing question: How did King Malcolm take this so easily? Here was the woman who had married Scotland's Chief of Chiefs drawing a steady stream of his subjects to her own independent court. Yet, in this he took only rest and encouragement for himself.

One night after Margaret had gone to bed with the children, she heard calls and clashes outside. Ah, they'd stayed too long at their ale again! It irked her how folk found these drunken stand-offs the highlight of all daily happenings. Were their smoky hearths and their productive toil such drudgery that to gather around two men blinder than bulls and watch them ruin each other stirred their highest passions?

Yet nothing brought people like a fight. And for days after two brutes fell upon each other, what talk was not of how they had clashed, who had offended whom and how, and what clans awaited another's apology before all the country should break out into war? They made epic songs to draw the tears of Scottish pride—all from such drunken dogfights.

Yes, and all the keening with the widow and orphans, and the generous filling of baskets and carrying them to the homes of the bereaved, where the curious could observe and gauge their suffering and their strength. No better chance for a woman to have her washing done! Nothing brought people together in such solidarity and charity as did a good killing!

The only action Margaret knew to take was to spare none of her attention for this fighting. She had determined to spend her energy rather on all the good yet to be known. So this night she turned over to sleep, like her babies.

But she was not yet asleep when servants pounded on her door.

"Queen Margaret! Queen Margaret! It's Fergus, slain by Mael Colum! They need you! They need you!"

Margaret pulled her tunic over her shift, tied back her hair, and put on a wimple. She buckled her belt and found her shoes. When she came out of the great hall doors, she found quite a dark night, with only the smudges of a few torches here and there to light the courtyard. She followed her men to the place where a fine, strong man lay still in the flickering dark. Why did she have to look at him? He twitched and shuddered in reflex, but his stillness was of death. A great cleft opened his shoulder, well down past his heart in his chest. The blood was a black pool under him.

Turgot was there, beginning the prayers for the dead. She knelt on the stones and prayed with them until he was finished.

At first she could not find Malcolm in the shadows. Then he came toward her, his face solemn in that strange look she knew as warrior's sorrow. Yes, there was devastation in his eyes, but also sheepishness. Presumption of sympathy. Pride, even, in having done what was hard to do but right. Affirmation of manhood.

Margaret wanted to spit on him.

She did not hold her arms out to him.

"His wife," she said, "is Bride, isn't she? Do they live up toward Edinburgh along the burn? Where is the chamberlain? Tell him to get good wine and our best bread and meat. Duthac, Moden, get horses ready, and men to go with me. We'll go to Bride."

It was bright morning when they returned. Margaret was so tired she told the chamberlain she had to sleep awhile.

She was already sitting on the bed in her shift when the words of St. Paul stopped her: "Do not let the sun go down on your anger."

Well, the sun had been already down, but now it was up. She pulled on her clothes again and went out to the hall to find her husband, still sleeping with his men. Squatting down, she shook his shoulder. She smoothed his hair back from his forehead and spoke near his ear.

"Mael Colum? Mael Colum?"

He rolled back his head to look at her.

"Mael Colum? I forgive you!"

"Fagh!" he said, and rolled his head away.

The days of mourning for Fergus kept a rock in her stomach. She had no sympathy for this needless death. Even the prayers of the Church stuck in her throat, for it seemed that the voices hers would join prayed these prayers with a certain relish—a call to God to take the blame for their own doing, a love of mourning, a satisfaction that this whole occurrence was something grand and beautiful.

She knew she was a hypocrite. How could she dare to judge another's soul? She could tell Jesus easily that she was so sorry about Bride and the children, and that he must use her to help them. She could easily pray that Fergus would rejoice in heaven. But she could not bring herself to love her life.

If she could not say good things, she had learned from her youth, she could say nothing at all. If she could not beam with happiness, she could smile and wish goodwill. *Acting* that way must soon make her *feel* truly that way. She carried herself quite graciously, and was solicitous of each one's needs, even Malcolm's. Her smile, however, took great effort. She did not smile one smile without giving herself the rational command to do so.

One day Malcolm came in from hunting and found her in the castle yard washing baby clothes. He was usually so full of good spirit when he came home from hunting, and she stood and made an effort to share his good feeling. Yet her smile was little more than a simper.

"That's the ugliest smile I've ever seen." Malcolm shouted. "Take it off your face. If you're happy, smile, and if you're not happy, don't!"

"Aye," she answered, "and if I don't smile just to suit your pleasure, will you cut me down as you did Fergus?"

He came close to her, his face glowing with rage.

"That is a most evil thing to say, Margaret! You know I have never touched you! I would never think of you hurtfully!"

"When you killed him, you killed me."

"I had no choice, Margaret. He challenged our clan. He'd undermined it!"

"Oh, you had no choice! You get up each morning with your mind already clear. Your body can almost lift a horse. You're the Chief of the Chiefs of Scotland. You had no choice?"

"It was the honor of the House of Dunkeld, Margaret. It was not only my fight. He would hurt us all!"

"The honor of the House of Dunkeld, was it? Honor? And God's honor? Where was the honor of God?

"God formed him and fashioned him, so tiny and right, in the womb—no one ever yet like him, nor yet will be. God carried him up to now, gave him growth and strength. Fergus loved the things that *you* love, Malcolm! If you were in the right mood, the two of you could have had a wonderful time on the moor or by the fire. God gave him Bride, his wife, and seven fine children to care for. And *you* cut him down, Malcolm, when God still wanted him to live. You may have sent him to hell!"

"He couldn't have gone to hell, Margaret—He died for honor. You can't understand. Will you *believe* that you can't understand? Can you trust that I might see things that you do not?"

"Honor! Man's honor I can't understand!"

"I hope you'll never see the day that will make you understand!"

Many had been working in the courtyard; indeed their two oldest children played with their nurse across the yard. All had slowed and stilled, trying to act as though they heard nothing, and yet unable to keep up ordinary talk, if only out of respect.

Margaret grabbed her arms to herself. She uttered the words evenly:

"I forgive you."

"Ah, you forgive me. The lily-white princess forgives me. I shall fly on my kilt!" And Malcolm left.

People marveled that he had not beat her.

Then Margaret saw herself and heard herself. She ran after him crying, "Forgive me, Mael Colum! Will you please forgive me?"

For days afterward he was morose, so that Margaret felt she had done great evil. He never came to their bed.

She did need his forgiveness. She had withheld her mind from him. She was wrong not to believe he could understand. She was cowardly not to have expressed her mind in peace. She had hurt him. Next time, she would take the right moment to share her mind with Malcolm, though softly. She would not be afraid, God help her.

During these days Margaret knew only to follow her rhythms of serving. The expected times for this and for that made it easier to begin. Then, once she met each person with his welcome and his need, she could put all her love into cleaning, feeding, bandaging, listening, and filling baskets to take on her visits. The worries of these people could occupy her mind.

How glad she was to have simple physical services she could do! A learned dissertation was like wood chips. She could hardly hold still to pray. Thank God no great feast had to be celebrated! She couldn't have cared if any of her fine nobles sat on the floor and ate nothing but the old rushes.

Her children she wanted to be with most of all. That was also hard. Little as they were, they knew she was sad. Though she chased them and captured them and juggled them laughingly, she still found herself often on the edge of tears. Taking them on her lap to teach them, as had been her custom, she could not do. The best times were when she and the children took some of the prankish young guard and went walking and playing in the fine countryside.

Malcolm never told her he forgave her. But one night he took her hand and came to bed. And he began to appear in the castle yard again when they served dinner to the destitute. He came more and more, until Margaret could know each day when he would be there. Now, he not only served food and played with babies. He cleaned tables, and he cleaned people. He would ask the one nearest him how he might help, and it seemed that whatever it was, he did it. Now he searched heads for scabies and cared for infections and sores. He would clean and so skillfully trim away dead flesh.

Now *that* was the way to use a blade.

18

The news came before the army returned from Abernathy. William held Duncan. The groups of defeated men began to straggle in, and they told of how their assault had been cut dead almost before it started. Always eager to lead, young Duncan was at the front, and was easily captured. Not one man had died protecting him.

As soon as King Malcolm learned that Duncan was taken, they said, he had ridden to find William. He had offered himself in his son's place, but had been refused. For any Scot to lift his hand further would have been the death of Duncan. Malcolm did well to come away from Abernathy with the terms he had: that he and William would desist from fighting right there, William keeping Duncan as surety of their peace.

Margaret went out to speak with the returning soldiers, learning their humiliation, but also, well-hidden, their relief. (So, beneath their fighting pride, these Scots did hold a desire to live? To love a family?) She was still with the men when, at last, at the end of his returning troops, came Malcolm. By the time she saw him she felt sick with anticipation. He did not relieve her. He took her full in his arms as always, but it was as though he embraced her in armor. He said little. The rest of that day he did all that a king returning from war must do, nothing more to Margaret than to anyone. Did he have anything more to say, or did he not know what he thought?

Anger was what she felt from him. Was it even anger at her?

Margaret for her part could hardly speak either. She could say she was sorry. That was true enough. She could not commend him or reassure him. What was this, to leave a son behind with a king ruthless enough to kidnap him? Yet, what else could Malcolm have done? He had saved a thousand men from dying. Was this not what she always begged of him?

Yes, but who was it brought on William's rage? Did they not both know, each time Malcolm left to raid a Norman post in Cumberland or North Umbria, that William would give them an answer?

These were the things of war, which Margaret had to trust to those who understood them. How sick every war cry made her. How dark she felt toward a man who would leave his son hostage! And yet, what was the death folk must live if their king did not continually fight back harassers? Did not scholarly men marvel that because of Malcolm's statecraft Scotland knew a peace beyond any in memory? Was this not the peace that enabled the rebirth of the Church and of the works of peace? Whenever she began to imagine what she would have done in Malcolm's place, Margaret came up short. The psalm sang for her, "I do not put my mind on things beyond my reach; I do not concern myself with matters too difficult for me."

When they came into their closet that first night Malcolm was home, she moved toward him quietly, but he turned from her. He did not find a reason to leave, but neither would he let her touch him. So they prepared for bed and went as they did on the nights when they were both very tired.

But lying here so made the tiredness grow! For long, she tried to think love.

I do love you, Malcolm, she breathed silently. *You are good.*

She stared into the dark.

I believe you are good. I know it. Who am I without you, Malcolm? You do not have to be good, Malcolm. I am not. I love you.

She lay still long.

God, let me love you!

Margaret reached her soul's hand out to Blessed Mary. *Help me, please*, she asked her. She held to Mary's hand, knowing that Jesus embraced them.

How icy it felt!

At last Margaret reached out her other hand, bodily, for her husband's shoulder. It was rigid and firm, not as in sleep. It did not move. But neither did it draw away. Margaret kept her hand on his shoulder. Slowly she moved closer, and slowly she fell asleep

As the days went by, Malcolm began to speak of what had happened. He let loose his rage. Easiest to blame was William. Sometimes he came close to putting his own self-blame into words. But, though not expressed in words, Margaret felt a sting to herself. She, who whittled away at a valiant heart, questioning, always questioning war! She, who never gave her husband that whole-hearted victory cry as he left to defend them. Did she not feel blame for confusing his judgment? Did she accept enough her guilt for garbling a true leader's purpose?

Duncan! Of this son left hostage would Malcolm never speak? Margaret herself felt such a cry in her heart! She missed him, and she grieved for failing him. How had she—with all the wise of Scotland—let such a youth go to defend them? All the boys younger than he who went each time, how did they let them go? Here was worry too great to hold, for how many—infants, nursing mothers, laughing children and fragile elders—would be ravaged if the young men stayed?

It was worse that Duncan was not her blood son. She did miss him sorely, and regret that she had shied away from him when he held himself aloof, as a youth will. But she slept and ate. If he had been born of her own body, would she have been able to sleep or eat? Did she love him *at all* more than from duty? Why was she so angry with Malcolm? Had she ever truly taken Duncan into her heart?

Of sons not born of her body, Lanfranc had said to expect these questions coming like demons, and to ignore them. Who can say he has loved enough? But it amazed her how the demons would slither in when the night was dark and still, or when some happening reminded her of Duncan.

Ingeborg, Margaret would pray, *you see I have lost this son of yours. You know if I ever held him close. Will you forgive me?*

I did have such hope, from that first day he taught me to play golf. When I pledged my troth to Mael Colum, your children were in my heart — Duncan most! We would build a bond, I was determined. ('determined.' Is that a word of love?) We did build a bond, Ingeborg. How closely we clung together when we lost his little brother! — Little Malcolm, your first son that I lost. Could he have lived if you had been here, and he felt his true mother's love? Could he have felt such love from me?

Yes, it is a waste to think these things. God saves us all!

But another thought she must open up with Ingeborg:

Why does Duncan always so fiercely want to prove himself to his father? Why does he always ride to the front? Does he want to be taken away? Does he want even to die? Does he live so strongly for his father and the realm, or is he only desperate to escape this life?

She asked Ingeborg's forgiveness, and she gave Duncan over to God.

Malcolm did not look at himself so closely, nor understand his moods — first anger, then kindness, then gloom, coming seemingly without reason. Margaret stayed near him, but felt she floated far from him. She could only watch and listen, to learn what she could do. Thus she helped bear Malcolm's nameless grief. Sometimes she had only to hold him and love him with all her might. Sometimes she would lie awake with him, or rise with him, and they would pass out by the castle guards and walk long in the black countryside. They might talk or they might not.

It was on one of these walks, when the wind whipped up from the dark sea and pulled at them screaming, and all heaven and the sea seemed to have forgotten their politeness to men, that Margaret had to ask him. She pulled herself up to his ear to make her question.

He slowed his walk and pulled her close.

"What is it now?" he called out.

"If I were in danger, only I, and you could save me by killing others, would you let them live?"

"If you were in danger? Do you think you're in danger?"

"No, Mael Colum, it's not that I'm in danger. I want you to promise that you wouldn't kill to save my life."

"You ask this tonight? You scream through a storm to ask me not to fight for you?"

She yelled back, "I've been thinking of it."

"So, if no one would die but you, would I hold back my hand?"

"Yes, no one but me."

"I cannot say," he yelled. "If it happened, I can't say what I'd do."

"You can!" she called back in his ear. "You can promise, and then you *will* know what you'll do!"

He had thoughts to tell, and here they were, fighting a storm! As they walked, he looked, until they came to a jumble of great rocks where he found a place somewhat sheltered.

"From all you've given me to know, I'd say I'd easily not fight if it were only for you," he told her, looking into her face, hidden in the dark except for the shining of her eyes. "But that would be only fear of your wrath. If I thought not of fear of you, and looked only at you, I'd slay whoever approached you."

"But you love me?"

"Aye, do you ask again?"

"And since you love me, you love to give me gifts?"

"I see where you're going."

"Nay, Mael Colum, it's not a trap. Truly, it's a gift I ask of you. You'd give me such joy with it!"

"I'll not promise it," he told her, holding his plaid around them. "But I'll hold it in my heart. I see it means much to you."

"Mael Colum," she kept on, "you could promise another gift."

"Tonight?" he answered.

"What if *you* were the only one whose life was threatened? Would you give your life, and not take the others'?"

"Would I hold back from protecting myself? If no one else would die? But what of you, left behind? What of my people? God gave them to me, you say it yourself!"

"God gave us to his Son, and his Son did not defend himself. It looked as if he left us behind."

"But, Margaret, He's God! He knew he did not really die!"

"Nay, Mael Colum, he did really die!"

"He did really die, but am I to rise from the dead and save Scotland? Nay, even more. I know if I die, I lose you."

"But you would have me so much closer, Mael Colum, though we know not how! Truly, too, you would do more for Scotland, with God's help."

"Well, it's easier, dear Margaret, to promise to let go of my life than to let go of yours. I can promise that."

So sometimes, in darkness and even wild weather, they found understanding and tenderness.

Yet Malcolm bound most of his feelings in hardness. He would treat her roughly for nothing, or fall into days of dejection. But Margaret was consoled that her interest in him did help to heal Malcolm. He did not strike out as people had known him to do before. Never in all the time of Duncan's exile did Malcolm take his grief into drunken oblivion.

The news of Duncan was, in fact, good. He sent a letter in his own hand, telling of a life akin to his father's when he had lived in the court of King Edward. (What a marvel was such a man as William that he should treat his hostage so agreeably! Had he no feeling of what an enemy is? Did he hold *anyone* in the world to be true foe or true friend? Were all merely pawns to be used as they were useful: treated kindly if not a threat?)

Time would slacken out, one year upon another. That Duncan lived as hostage would become familiar. Raw knowledge would wear smoother. Though news would continue to be of opportunities and enterprises Duncan enjoyed like an honored guest, never would there be assurance of his safety. And steadily Malcolm would strain against his bonds, keeping his spies circulating and watching with his council to find a way with William.

The year 1072 did not bring only the defeat and sorrow of Abernathy. It was in that same year that the Norsemen who ruled from the Orkneys returned the isle of Iona to the people of Scotland.

19

ona! This was the island where Christ had been born for Scotland! Who had not heard of it in story and song? Yet it had become a place only of memories—a place of buried kings. The rocks of it were black with the ocean spray and mist. Still bearing up against wind and spray and lichen, these stones were the ones that had not yet fallen. Dark they were, and they held a silence of a life that had been—of men moving about here daily, building, working, singing God's praises. Margaret, as she stopped by Malcolm once they had stepped free of the sea water, knew that the silence was not only of a life that had been. The life was here still. She felt the spirits who still dwelt here. She did not talk, and she walked carefully, in reverence to them. Malcolm kept silence with her.

How did you live? she breathed to those monks of those lost ages. *What is there here? What meager plants! Were you ever warm from the time you waded up these banks? The howling and tearing of the wind! How could you sleep unless you were deadly exhausted?*

They walked first to Relig Oran, where rows of sleeping stone warriors marked the burial places of generations of chieftains and kings. Malcolm's father Duncan lay here, and so, too, did Malcolm's victim MacBeth. Malcolm knelt at his father's grave, and in sorrow at the grave of MacBeth, with Margaret beside him. They moved to the resting places of Kenneth MacAlpine and of other men Malcolm admired and lived to emulate. He who was usually to be seen taking matters into his own hands knelt as a humble vassal, honoring and waiting to hear.

They found where the church must have been. Here Margaret prayed as a pilgrim, praising God for all he had done here, and asking fellowship with all who had served him here. She begged to give God what he would like for this place.

From the church they walked what they could find of the old floors. They traced out what must have been passages and rooms used for different purposes. The monks who accompanied them could surmise from their own experience how things must have been laid out, though only roughly, for this place of prayer had begun long before the monastic customs they now practiced. Columkille and his monks had at first had only little stone hermitages, a little cluster of hovels.

But many had been called here since then, and this place had teemed with activity. It had been an awesome site of pilgrimage. People heard of the life of Iona and made their way across land and water to dwell for a while at this gate of heaven. What a beautiful church they'd found, and filled many hours of the day with the sacred singing of the monks! Pilgrims had gentle welcome from these men who were so strict with themselves. Visitors rested like children in the guest house, being served the good, simple food. They had opened their hearts to fathers worn and humbled in God's service.

Even one who came not for God would have marveled at the finely worked crosses, the refined stonework, and the rich crafts of the monks. They would have seen the pages of the great book that was now kept safe at Kells—that legendary volume of the Gospels illuminated with unearthly brilliance in color and gold.

Those years of daily peaceful routines, though, seemed lost under the last human activity these pillars and walls had seen. How had it been, that last time the huge men from the North had swarmed up the bank? Armored men they were, sporting dreadful trophies of war and carrying hideous weapons. They came wild-eyed after long winter months confined in dark huts, hungry and angry from enduring the sea, lusting for plunder and for stories of valor to take home to their gatherings. Time and again they had come, sometimes holding back at the sight of such defenseless men. At last they had torn into the monastery with pure fury, leaving nothing but smoking, fallen walls and bloodied, broken bodies.

Two hundred seventy years ago that had been, and in those two hundred seventy years, to try to settle new monks on that desolate isle was not to be considered. Hard enough the life there had always been, and then the Vikings had taught them well that they would punish whoever tried to stay. The only pilgrimages had been the funeral processions of chieftains and kings—even of Norsemen. Dead, they were safe there with all the leaders of old.

But now the men of the North gave Scotland peace and protection. Men like Thorfinn of Orkney kept their countrymen in hand. The battling and bargaining, the alliances and intermarriage, and, too, the gentle breath of the Gospel had borne fruit.

There were many sites in Scotland more fitted than the Isle of Iona to living and growing food: green, rich hills with fine burns and springs; country soft in the spring and hot in the summer, not far from the beaten road, so that goods could be carried back and forth, and pilgrims come with ease. But Iona was the birthplace of the Church for the Scots. When again bells rang in its church tower and monks' sandals shuffled daily on its floors, a hole in the heart of the Scots Church would be healed, and new strength and confidence would beat.

Margaret and Malcolm stayed on the isle a few days asking God to help them to see. The abbot who had been assigned to make this foundation planned with the master builder who had come with them. Then they returned to Dunfermline and the lands where they would find all they needed to re-establish Iona. In not too long Margaret would make one more trip across Scotland, to worship as queen at the first Mass to be celebrated in the new Iona monastery.

20

alcolm had declared his pure heart toward Margaret, but he could yet be turned. One thing she did rankled him. Down in the rock not far east of the castle was a cave she had found. Often, when she could, she would go off to it to be alone. The first time, she had asked him. He had not questioned her going. She sought many things that he would not have thought of, but she had her own good reasons. After Margaret had gone to the cave a few times, it became habit. She might tell one of her ladies when she went, or if she couldn't be found, it was sure that she was in the cave.

Feeding the poor and visiting homes and sitting on a rock listening to people were activities that everyone beheld. But this seeking solitude, even beyond the chapel: what drove her? In those insecure times, people found their life together. They were used to others snuffling next to them in sleep; they thought of a meal more as companionship, as serving and being served, than as eating. To go off alone was a very different thing. One who did this must not care about his safety, and if he went willfully, it was usually for strong ascetic or spiritual reasons—or for deeds of darkness.

Margaret's time in the castle chapel mystified Malcolm, but he had found her there the first morning after she had come to Dunfermline. He had learned to know her as one who spent long times there. That was seemly, too, for one who loved God. The place was built securely within the fortress enclosure. It was fitted with prayerful things: the altar, the cross, holy vessels, and the Scriptures; pictures and symbols of the Lord and his mother. Its narrow benches forced your soul to hold up your body. It was made to be a little desert in the midst of the crowd.

So, why did one need to slink off to some more remote place in the name of prayer?

Was Margaret pining? Did she despise his house, and only feign happiness? Could she be losing her mind? She would not be the first in this dim, high country, especially with all her early risings and exhausting occupations.

Yet her face did not look at all vacant or forced. How would it feel to be as happy as she looked? A great, hot cloud slid up the back of his neck. There was a way a person became that radiant...

Malcolm shrugged off his doubt and came more often to help her with the lowly ones. Surely she could not have much more energy when she was finished with them? And their smell. Would she go off to an assignation smelling so? Still he studied faces round the court for one who might have her heart. At dinner, where did she glance most lightly? Was she looking beyond her cup when she toasted? Did she dance with any more gladly than with others?

Yet, why need he be so covert? *She* openly and easily left and returned. He could just as easily go after her to the holy cave.

That day the forsythia was blooming sweet, and every bush was popping with bright green, swelling buds. The sunlight was not full but fitful, as though a moving cloud could pull it away or bring it again. The road was dark with new mud and hard to walk in, but one could walk easily on the grassy berm. Tiny birds tried out their new spring songs. One great, dark bird floated silently overhead.

Malcolm did not notice what was young or sweet or beautiful. He noticed what made noise and what kept quiet; what was in shadow and what blended easily with the green.

He followed the road down to where it turned and saw the hole in the green that was the cave entrance. No good resting place showed itself just across from it, so he backtracked and saw that he could climb onto the swell that made the cave's roof. His climbing loosed pebbles and snapped branches, but he was heedless as he settled himself comfortably under some bushes growing right over the cave entrance. Let her wonder! Let her wait long to find who might be visiting her door.

He himself waited long. He heard nothing but the sounds of the green. Some small stream, too, must be flowing in the cave. Not a person came or went. Not a word or a song touched the air. In the drowsy sun he might have had to fight sleep, if he had not had a stronger interest to keep him alert.

A group of young boys rollicked past on their way to fish. A tired old man plodded up the hill with his catch.

Still the cave was silent, and no one entered or left.

At last, as the abbey Angelus bells subsided, she passed out the entrance as lightly as a shadow and hurried up the road. He waited until she must have reached the castle, and gingerly stretched his cramped limbs. He dropped to the cave's doorway, bent his head, and walked in. The place was about eight feet by twelve, and high enough that Malcolm could stand comfortably in it. The walls were of a pale, sandy stone, and the back wall was wet with seepage. A trickle slid down its tiny course to a little pool. Though the cave seemed dark, it was open to the setting sun, softly warming the walls with rose color. There was no seat or shelf or furniture of any kind. There were no stores of food or drink. There was no cross, nor any religious sign.

Malcolm left and went back to the castle quietly.

Another day he followed Margaret and stood openly at the cave door. No response came from within. He bent his head enough to lean in out of the sunlight and see in the dimness. Margaret sat back on her heels on the cave floor, close to one side wall and facing the other. Her eyes were closed; her face was still; her hands lay folded in her lap. There was nothing and no one else in the cave.

A soft wonder and a warm joy rose in him, warming even his shame.

"Margaret?" he whispered. "My pearl of great price!"

Her eyes opened and she rose gladly to come to his side.

"Oh, you are too good for me," he whispered tight against her head. "Your secrets are *always* too good! Margaret, I doubted you. I couldn't believe you could find enough that was interesting in this solitary place. Will you forgive me, Margaret?"

Margaret was lithe and light in his arms. She raised her eyes to his. "Will you pray with me, Mael Colum?"

Softly she pulled him down to kneel beside her. After some time she touched him to come with her. "Please, Mael Colum, come whenever you will and pray with me here. What a joy it was to see you leaning in this door!"

She kissed him with such longing. He twirled her around, and pulled her running up the hill.

Malcolm called his mormaer, who called carpenters, farriers, and workers in fine metal, and fine seamstresses, too. Before Margaret, the king ordered them to fit that cave well as a proper chapel. No effort or skill was to be spared. Malcolm's bluff good cheer helped to shave away the scum of his guilt.

Margaret agreeably sat with the artisans, conferring on how to furnish the cave as a beautiful chapel. In herself, she was amazed at how deeply Malcolm's doubt scored her heart. If she had cast herself on God's love alone, how could this pain be so sharp? Malcolm was only used to common expectations. Even holding her in highest regard, how could he not wonder according to his own experience? His own experience? What might she, Margaret, wonder of him during all those days he was gone on war and state business?

Fitting out this chapel ... Were not those smooth, blonde walls, sometimes bathed in sun, always safe from rain, the most perfect chapel? Was there not the tiny rivulet in springtime, feeding into the still, small pool? Always was that place hidden and still. Did she need a bench and a kneeler, wrought iron and candlesticks and a cross?

Yes, she could pray with all these things as well as without them. Perhaps she had clutched this hidden place to herself. Now it might draw many to commune with their Lord. Her husband most of all. For it was exactly by providing the furnishing, seeing her care to make it most beautiful, and watching over his gift that he seemed his most free, true self.

Indeed, to decorate and embellish the things Margaret treasured was Malcolm's natural way to free his love. There had been the time when her Gospel book was not on its stand. A thing of such honor, kept in an honorable place, could only have been taken willfully. All knew that it was a work of thousands of hours for the scribes; that it was one of the most valuable things for its weight that could be had. Margaret had made known humbly that it was gone, and had taken the days quietly, hoping that someone would answer her. She had resolved not to rouse a fierce search. The book was a means of good to whoever had it. Let God see that it came to the right hands.

Then Malcolm had slipped into her room one early evening, knelt close to her feet as she sat, and taken from his cloak a great package wrapped in velum. He placed it in her lap, and she folded back the wrapping. In the candlelight glinted the deep, clear colors of true jewels and the gloss of burnished gold. She saw that the jewel work outlined the familiar design of the cross engraved on her Gospel book. Here was her book, highlighted and ornamented with the finest gold work!

Kneeling on the floor close to her, Malcolm looked up at her much as a young boy might. He could hardly contain his self-satisfaction at the joy he offered her. He must not see that regret fought with joy in her heart! It *had* entered her mind that Malcolm might be the thief. A wisp of hope had kindled that he was secretly learning to read. But no, it was not the treasure within the book that he longed for, but to praise this woman who treasured it. What he could give her was pure, fine-worked gold, and jewels imported from afar. How much had this cost her people? And that not a feather-weight to the value of the Life borne by the words within the book! And what had it cost the king? A few moments of giving an order.

Like a child, Jesus says, see me. No stipulations. See in any gift the one who gives. See Malcolm. Here, in the finest treasures of earth, glimmers his heart. All hers—and all his own. How could she thank him enough?

Malcolm would often take a book that he knew she loved and commission rich decoration for it. But he gave not only flamboyant gifts. Though he never aspired to read, Margaret found him at times sitting quietly, holding one of her books as she did. It reminded her of herself when she had been four or five, and had asked her mother for a prayer book like hers. Her mother had given Margaret a small one, light enough to carry. Though not a mark on the page meant a thing to her, Margaret had taken it to Mass and knelt holding it exactly as the nuns did, speaking the words she knew by heart, and every so often turning a page.

Yet Malcolm was not imitating her. He was treasuring her in the book. She could clasp the book to herself as she would Malcolm.

21

unfermline Abbey had a room with one great table, where the monks would meet in chapter. It was to this table that Margaret and the bishop from London invited all the priests of Scotland who could come. After days of the king's hospitality, resting and feasting, they could accept a few hours of sitting to a table so stark.

Even after five hundred years of the Gospel, these men whose only work was the Peace of Christ seemed somewhat strange to most Scots. Most of them had spent some years studying in France or England, or at least in a monastery. Beyond the teaching of Rome, they were acquainted with the cultural heritage of the Holy Roman Empire. Yet the peat smoke ran deep through their veins. They were proud Celts. Their people demanded that they be. It was their people they loved, and they had no doubt that Christ, too, was a Celt.

Over the years they had assumed more of a Gaelic way of doing things, so that a pilgrim from Rome might not be able to follow their Mass. Some of the Scots customs were not even discernible from those of the Druids. The priestly tonsure, for instance, was not the crown form of Europe, but the ear-to-ear form, precisely of a Druid. Most folk could not see that such things were here or there, since God was at the heart, but Bishop Lanfranc led those who saw that without carefulness in the signs, they were losing the Truth.

Margaret had intuitions about these things that made her summon scholars who could transmit the customs of the One Church clearly and explain them. Her part was to entertain and cherish all who came, and to go out with the bishop to those who could not come.

Now that these gathered shepherds had spent a day in discourse, Margaret, seated beside the king, begged to address them.

"My dear Fathers, I have prayed long that King Malcolm and I might have you as our guests. God has entrusted to us the care of all of the clans of Scotland. You know I was not born on this soil, but when I married my king, God gave me a heart that belongs to Scotland more than if I had been born here. Peace and health and prosperity for all in this land—this is our sacred commission.

"By God's grace almost all of our people have found their spiritual home in Christ's Church. The Church is our soul. The soul is where we begin when we want health for the body. So, more than any effort we make for the rights and peace of each man and woman to make a family and prosper together, we must have strength and purity in the Church.

"You know and I know that many a man who sits here has had to overcome himself to come to this table. This people north of Britain has never been conquered. Often we have been assailed, but the Romans finally had to build walls to protect Britain from us, and the Norsemen have retreated to small isles. Among ourselves we refuse to be conquered. We are not so much one people as seventy clans, each proud and strong in itself. The drive that has kept us strong is of stubbornness against all. It is a great and beautiful stubbornness, which can polish each clan against the other to shine with hard luster. But there is One whom we must let conquer us. He conquers us by letting us nail him to the cross. This gentle Savior conquers not to destroy, but to free us for all good.

"As your queen, dear Fathers who are sons, I ask you one thing: Look on Christ. The customs you are addressing may seem small or not pertinent, but we look at them only because of Christ who has loved us. He is all that matters.

"You are each Christ. *In persona Christi Capitus* you act, as priests. You strain with all your lives to be one with that man, Son of God, sacrificed for us. No other purpose would make sense of the strange lives you lead.

"You cannot look upon him enough, pinned open on the cross in obedience to his Father. We pinned him there. We ourselves cannot stand such pure obedience.

"Christ willed to be *Capitus, Head* of a Body made of all men. His Body, he tells us, is this Church, and we believe him. One Body. He dwells on this earth in one Body. It's this oneness we pursue in official signs, and in the sacred Mystery of the Eucharist, which we are commissioned to hold up as a candle. The oneness of the signs must be exact, to protect our own weakness and because we are custodians of a Gift, a mystery of which we have no comprehension. These days, the head of his Body on earth has spoken for his bishops that these matters of protocol are not to be taken into men's own hands.

"You Celts, and I, too, if only a Saxon, bear great pride. We will not be subjugated. Christ will not abide either, that we be subjugated. He asks that we subjugate ourselves.

"He shows us how to do it. Did he, the great God, Creator of Creation, choose to come among men as a Pict? No, for then some might have been in awe of him. He came as one of a tiny, whining race always kicked around the eastern desert.

"He has, in fact, let it be that the language of oneness in his Body, now stretching across the world, is the language of the race that pulverized his own! It is the language in which he was condemned to death. As a man, if he still walked the earth unglorified, would this not choke in his craw?

"But he has seen this way to be good for his Church.

"Why did Jesus care to make sure he was of no account? Why does he allow that all the truth he has given is carried in the forms of people's customs—from one culture to another, so that no one can bow to him without bowing to ways of doing things that he finds alien—that he, in fact, may despise? Because we must awaken to what it means that 'there is not either Jew or Greek, male or female, slave or free. We are one in Christ.' These words are a great mystery for each of us, though we repeat them as though we understand.

"If I bend my will to this or that custom, to this or that language, the custom and language dissolve away to reveal Christ. He shows himself to me. I see only him.

"Two of the calls you are receiving from Bishop Lanfranc reach far deeper than custom. Keeping the Lord's Day sacred is one of God's Ten Commandments. We all have the wolf at the door. We feel that God would not give us opportunities to get work done if he did not want us to use them. But only a God of love would command us to take a whole day every seventh day and rest from all but God's Work—the Eucharist of our Redemption. In the Mass he will give us power far beyond what we can make and do. And he knows that unless we can trust him enough to hand our lives over to him each First Day, we cannot break into friendship with him. That is all God wants. As he makes each man, he waits for his close friendship.

"Another conversion required of you wrenches your very heart—your priestly vow not to marry. Our people find it so strange that any man should take all his passion away from the marriage bed and to the altar. How can you defend your manliness to your people? And yet, this is the way Christ chose. Is he a whole man? These commands that pitch us hardest against our understanding—must they not bring us very close to God, who is beyond all understanding?

"The extra burden for you who have already taken women and begotten families, and must now change your relations with them—the king and I will see that with the Church we help you provide for your obligations. Have faith, I ask you.

"As to the other directives our bishop is presenting to you: God asks us to do hard things—to fight pride, covetousness, lust, anger, gluttony, envy, sloth. To be faithful in family life, to forgive and speak peace—most of all, to love! These are hard to things to hold fast to. But the *easy* things are how you shave your head, what manners and words you use in the Mass, how much more readily you allow your flock to receive Jesus in the Eucharist. These are nothings.

"We look at Jesus, simple and naked in love, and we want to do these little things so perfectly, that we may be faithful in great ones.

"You have my gratitude and my prayers as your humble queen, dear Fathers. Your Chief of Cheifs, Mael Colum Canmore, and I take deep joy in having you with us here, and in all that you will accomplish with God."

More such meetings would follow, with the sparks of outrage and resentment flying up on the paths leading to them, and mostly dying during the priests' time together, so that they rode back to their parishes with clearer resolve and a strange warmth of peace. Not always were the meetings at Dunfermline, but sometimes at the monastery being restored at Iona. There, in the beautiful chapel rebuilt on the place where Christ had first come to Scotland, they knew in the Liturgy the presence of the many who had lived and died before them there, only for the Lord.

And to those in the far distant clans, Margaret herself traveled with those who would teach them.

f all schools of prayer which had sprung up around the land in these last years, the shrine which meant the most to all Christians in Scotland was the church of their patron, St. Andrew, at Edinburgh. No one but knew of it, and the stories of what St. Andrew had done for them. But it was not a place that drew many people. For one thing, there was the Firth of Forth to cross. A ferry was not always handy, and many could not pay the fare. It took determination to make the trip there, and find a place to camp.

Jesus had said that no one needs to go to this or that holy mountain to worship well, but can worship within himself, in spirit and truth. He had often told his disciples not to look in ethereal places to find God, for the Kingdom of God is among us. Yet, Jesus had made the lawful pilgrimages to Jerusalem each year. He had often settled himself by the Temple to teach. When he knew it was time for his Sacrifice, he had set his face for Jerusalem.

Margaret had seen both in Hungary and in England how people take inspiration from making pilgrimage to a revered place. To focus on one place that spoke of God and to rouse themselves to travel there helped them treasure God in their midst. Most people had little time to refine the arts of beauty, but some must make that their devotion. Some must do that here at St. Andrew's! They must build and adorn a place to reflect God's beauty. Then all their brothers and sisters could come to take rest and be lifted toward God. Handing over their survival to God for a few days, they could put their hearts on his Word, on his Sacrifice, on all the powers he has put in creation. They could be fed at his Table in this lofty place, and then return to serving him, humble and hidden, with the images of that pilgrimage to bear them up and show them the truth of their lives.

This place of pilgrimage must not only be orderly and beautiful. It must be a home where anyone could find welcome. Being received with joy, being taken in and cared for, side by side with your brothers and sisters—this healed a person and showed him God. So St. Andrew's must be the home of the kindest and most gentle monks.

Again Margaret went to Father Turgot for help to find a good father to the community at St. Andrew's. She showed Malcolm how it might be good for the unity of all Scotland if the seat of their king were also the seat of their heavenly patron. So he had Edinburgh Castle trimmed and cleaned, and rebuilt for the needs of his court, and he and Margaret moved their family to Edinburgh. Now it took folk only one trip to come to God or to come to their queen. Margaret could walk often at St. Andrew's with the monks and the pilgrims from across the country. So close was their home to this holy shrine that people who came felt the life and hospitality of the royal family.

Now Margaret must ask for gifts to endow this place. There must be room and comfort for guests. A fine ferry must transport them. (*Queen's Ferry* it came to be called.) No fees must be asked for any of it. Those who had taken healthily from the earth could secretly put into the pot for those who held back out of need. Then, without distinction, all could come together to the house of St. Andrew, the saint who kept Scotland in his lap.

Edinburgh became a place folk looked to if they wanted to learn. A young girl or a young man could speak to the parish priest about going to a convent or monastery school. There was help to support them there. Scholars, both women and men, came to stay for a time, speaking in the schools and teaching in Margaret's court. What had seemed not worth considering showed itself fascinating and to be pursued.

People would bring their finest dye work and weavings to the market, where others would be inspired to improve on them. Metalwork, needlework, even little-known arts and crafts, would come to the market or be brought as gifts to Queen Margaret. Folk would see them and be no longer satisfied with what they themselves had made. They would seek teachers, or they would intensify what they did themselves, until they could vie with fine artisans. So, not only did groups gather to learn from skilled artisans, but wool and the products of Scotland became much sought after elsewhere. The Scots had hard work to meet the demand. Then many a weaver or a crofter found he had traded for more than he'd ever had, so he could buy more and better, not only for his work, but for his family to live. There was work for more people, and more to eat. And all about Edinburgh—it was the talk of the wide countryside—people walked about wearing bright colors!

But Edinburgh was not the castle of Dunkeld. Dunfermline, lone and free on the high, rocky point, was still the place that Malcolm and Margaret's family found home. It was home to Malcolm especially, and he said he hoped they would bury him there, close to the wind and the sea.

23

Mary sat, breathing hard, leaning against the cool wall behind her, and watching the spectacle of light and color moving before her to the tune of pipes, harp, and strings—just a moment or two to catch her breath before this dance ended. The hall was the greatest room she had ever been in, a lofty space full of air—with a ceiling so high that smoke and darkness rose up above the glint and sparkle and warm colors of hundreds of people in gracious dance. The light of the hearth fires and the thousand tiny points of candles glimmered, wavered, and flowed in and out of the whirls of movement: Faces flashing by too quickly to take them in. Bodies lithe and joyously free. Costumes so rich and original, draped or pulled tight, shining or velvety, in colors brilliant or soft or dramatic. Swift precision of moving designs formed by men and women watching, stepping, side-stepping, twirling, coming close and then moving away. The cares of survival, the labors of the day, and the tensions of living close to one another— all were dissolved in music and laughter and grace.

Mary watched Queen Margaret as she now danced close to her. She wore a dress of deep blue-green, like the depths of the sea, over a pale blue linen shift. The fit of the shift beneath the cutaway dress was close, except where its sleeves fell, long, open, and flowing, longer than the tips of her fingers if she let her arms down. The dress fit closely along her breast and smoothly to the silver belt at her hips, where it flared softly, swirling as she moved in the dance. Her coif was not of a heavy cloth, but of a fine, light silk that showed the shining, braided honey-golden coils beneath it. How smooth her face looked, though so radiant with the dancing, the warmth, and the merrymaking. The color was concentrated in two rosy spots high in her cheeks; her eyes were brilliant blue, reflecting the blue of her dress.

Now she danced with the Earl of Fife, MacDuff, the king's good friend. She did not fear to give him her full, pure smile, and he returned it. Soon she would be back in the arms of the king— often she came back to him—and that dancing would be the most beautiful to behold. Malcolm might be thought to be too strong for such a light lady, but he knew her so well, and he watched her so closely. Her eyes never left his as they danced, and he seemed to be the strength beneath her light leaps and twirls. Their dance was not spectacular; it was only so free and graceful and full of spirit. It pulled those around them into the same joy and lightness.

The next day, Mary and Queen Margaret sat pushing their silk-threaded needles in the quiet of a balcony's daylight. Since Mary had come to learn at King Malcolm's court, now almost two years ago, this needlework had become a habit of most days. Usually a group of ladies gathered together, but today all but she and the queen were decorating and making gifts for a feast for the children.

"You love parties, don't you, my queen?" Mary asked.

"I do, sweet Mary," the queen replied.

"You're not afraid to dress richly for them, are you, though you're said to be so spiritual? And you use such fine manners."

"Aye, Mary," said the queen, "why should I fear to dress richly and use fine manners? Parties are a foretaste of heaven, you know? Blessed be God; He gives us parties all through life to keep reminding us—to show us a peek of what our life here hides.

"And I'm Scotland's queen. Together, the king and I should be the best partiers in the land. All should be able to look to us to see how it's done! We make an art of richness and fine manners, all in the name of our people."

"You don't fear the people, my Lady?" Mary asked. "Many there are, you know, who take your fancy ways hard. The true, good Scot, they say, is simple and pure. He does not need contrived colors and styles, materials, and foods and manners. He sees it as it is, and he loves it as it is."

"Do you think our festivities are not true, Mary?"

"Do I, Your Highness? Ah, I love them, and I see no pretense. A bright color or a gracious manner is as real as a crude one. No, I love these intense hours. But folk would say, you know, that nothing's real but what's real for a poor man."

The queen pulled another strand of silk through her needle's eye.

"True," she said. "In some way those folk are right. But how does the poor man find a better life? By all making their lives as poor and drab as the poorest?

"No, to give good one must culture good. If a person has discovered more of the wealth that's hidden for men to find, not only can he share what he has found, but in having it he lets others behold it and strive for it. And I think, Mary, that leaders give their people joy and hope when they show them loveliness and culture.

"Culture is a human gift, you know. The animals take the earth as it is, but God wants us men to be creators. He gives us the raw material and says, 'Fill the earth and subdue it.' He gives us the grace of art—to make something *better* of what he has made! Can you believe it?"

"So you're not afraid of offending your people, my Lady?"

"Aye, Mary," the queen smiled, "I hope I do not. I must go gently, listen to them; listen to God in my heart, for he tells me if I'm serving myself. But I would be a coward, Mary, lazy and stingy, not to develop what I know to be so good, only from fear of criticism!"

They both sewed for a time. Mary was not to be here much longer, and here she had Queen Margaret to herself.

"You do like the wine, my Lady," Mary said. "You like to try different kinds. And you like the beautiful clothes—and the dancing—and the light and clever talk. You are not just performing out of duty."

"Oh, yes, Mary. I do love it all!" answered the queen. "They're good! God made them good. How can I not enjoy them?"

"But then, my Lady, after that late dancing, you rose this morning in the dark to pray like a nun in the cold chapel."

Margaret laughed. "Like a nun? Nuns are not the only people God waits for. God waits for me, Mary, each morning, and I long to go and be still with him. He waits for you, too."

"So early in the morning, my queen?"

"No, maybe not so early in the morning. Do you know, some people he waits for in the night—or even in the afternoon! Me he waits for early in the morning.

"First, I am only still, to praise him. Then I look toward the Mass. Parties are a foretaste of heaven? The Mass *is* heaven!

"*Can* I be ready for Mass? Who can? I could take a lifetime and not be ready for it, or God could make me ready for it in an instant. But I have time. Many people have to work so hard that they don't have time to prepare for Mass. I have time. The Church has its great prayer: the Divine Office, God's Work. I join in that prayer, and it carries me into Mass, and again carries me out with the Mass."

"Do you know what I think, my Lady?" said Mary. "Since you let me tell you what I think—I think that you push the life of a queen and the life of a nun into one life. And more than that. You schedule your whole day like you were a page in training. You must always feed your nine infants before your breakfast, and then at midday you and the king have your three hundred vagabonds to dinner. In the afternoon you put on your hood and ride out to your stone to listen. Each day you have your hours with your children, playing with them and teaching them. If they do not each become skilled in the highest things, and, I think, if they do not love Christ very much, you will take it hard against yourself. And all of each day you have your twenty-four destitute companions. "It's at least three lives you're pushing into one. I wonder if you are a heroic saint? Or could you be a fanatic, and one of these days you will completely lose your mind?"

They sewed quietly. Then Margaret spoke.

"You are asking me these things, Mary, because you want to know for your own heart? For how you will live? For how you will find Jesus?"

"Aye, my Lady," Mary answered softly. "I have much to think about with you. Soon I will be back in my father's house, and what will I take with me? Even in my own family who sent me here, they say either that you are a mystic saint, carried by angels, or that you are unhinged, and someday will fly completely off the handle. But I see so much wonderful here, and I don't think it's magic. You are happy. I want to know: Are you like me? Am I like you?"

"I will tell you about the putting three lives together, Mary. People have asked me something like that before. It could seem so, glancing from one person to another. But it is very simple. Jesus lets *me* know what he wants me to do, and he gives me what I need to do it. I can do nothing without him. No one can. So, *how much or how little* someone does is not of interest. God sends me. He has work for me. As I do it, I lack for nothing.

"I hope to do no more than he asks. It's not only that I don't want to do wrong things. Even things that may be good in themselves, I do not want to do unless he wants me to. If I can do this, I will not be tired or worn.

"You are right, it's not a charmed life. Why would God deprive me of working? You see how the squires are, after years of training, how free and strong their bodies are, how much more they are themselves? When I work with God, I help him, and I hatch myself.

"I do not often see or feel that I have what I need, either. It is faith. I know my Beloved will give me every good thing; most surely my needs. Not knowing how I can do it, I do much simply in trust of my Beloved. Isn't that what makes love sweet?"

Margaret held her pattern out to measure the stitches.

"What God gives me, and what God wants from me, Mary, will be different than what he wants for you. It's true, you don't figure out God's will from nothing. Much we all have in common: the Ten Commandments; the Gospel; the Church's light. I have patterned my life on other lives, too, and so learned what fit me. I come to my confessor like a child, to submit all I do to God. I go after things, and he speaks for God, showing when I must drop one thing or pick up another.

"My military scheduling. Why do I have such set daily plans? I'll tell you why it's for my people, and I'll tell you why it's for me.

"A queen can be kept from her people. She can be far within the castle, with so many administrators to help her that when one of her subjects comes to see her, he must begin by explaining himself to the gatekeeper, and then, if the gatekeeper lets him go by, he must justify himself to a whole chain of authorities until, if he has convinced all of these, he might be shown in to Her Formal Highness. But what more is she than a mother? Perhaps she would love to have this son or daughter of hers happen in and lighten her day. How is she to know who needs her the most, and how are they to know if she wants to be with them?

"If a queen and king are in custom of being available for certain reasons at certain times of each day, and it is well known, then all can find us. Whatever their business is, they will not feel exceptional. If certain numbers become custom, then nothing else determines whether someone stays away or not. If all know that I take nine babies each day, then nothing decides who comes and who does not, save counting to nine. Those more than nine on one day will be one of the nine the next day. If all know that from two o'clock to three o'clock each afternoon, I sit on my stone to meet with any who come, no one is offended when it is three o'clock. They await their turn in due course.

"I give you another reason for ordered scheduling. War and disaster are never far from us. If they do come, a firm structure of happenings gives us all a peacefulness; a framework to hold onto and build from. Maybe we do not have enough protection, or food, or water, or materials to work, but if we know that the queen shall be welcoming the usual people at the usual times, and that there are certain routines of serving, educating, and crafting which steadily continue, we calm ourselves and see much that we can do.

"Ah, Mary, how sure I am: To starve war, feed peace! The more valuable a life people have developed, the less willing they become to sacrifice it to war."

Queen Margaret put down her work, and, seeing this, Mary did so, too. Margaret took her hand.

"But the reasons for such steady days are not the reasons of my heart. It is *I* who need them, Mary. Do you know why it is?

"I want to follow where my spirit wants to go. My flesh does not understand this. My flesh wants to roam alone or to relax in comfort with people I consider intelligent, sensitive, clever—people who titillate and tantalize me—people who hold me in high regard. My spirit knows that the strong hands that will pull me to God are those of the forgotten, the unheard, the uncouth.

My flesh wants to scorn those people we call poor, especially when they scorn me. I would run from them every chance I had, unless I scheduled my life with them, like the waves of the sea. Other interests would press me, until many days would pass without me even seeing these most important people in the world. The more I am forced to welcome them, the more I begin to understand and maybe even become gracious with them. My flesh wants earthly light and color; it wants order and cleanliness and earthly freedom. It resents that where there is life, there's a mess.

"Habit gives my spirit advantage over my flesh. It takes me daily to those dearest to Jesus. Then, though I *feel* him not at all, there is Jesus, looking at me from saucy, belligerent, or dull eyes. Then I reach for his garment, like the bleeding woman, and I take him in my arms, and he holds me."

24

wenty-one years after he had conquered England, in the
same month, William the Bastard died in Normandy
while fighting to retrieve what he had lost there. It was
September 1087. His second son, William Rufus (*the Red*), took the
English throne. Duncan was twenty-seven when he came home
again to Edinburgh. First the homecoming feast, and then he again
lived at home. Margaret and Malcolm thanked God.

Yet, it was strange to be together after such a span of time. They
came up against one another often, and could have lost faith but for
the bond they knew they must fulfill. As they worked through each
day, moments came when each would recognize the person they had
known, understanding now as never before.

Soon they sent Edith and David, of their own free will, to the
court where Duncan had been held by force. David was nine and
Edith ten when they left to learn the ways of chivalry in William II's
queenless court, and to be near Bishop Lanfranc. Now only Mary,
the youngest, remained with her parents.

Even as they sent their son and daughter in peace to the court of
the English king, Malcolm knew that raids and treacheries increased
south of them, and that it was William behind them. Soon Rufus
was openly raging into North Umbria, punishing and laying waste
villages, monasteries, and farmlands without distinction. Leaving
whole swaths of land dead and black, he pushed aggressively north.

Duncan must again be off to fight, with his father and brothers. As the newly-gleaned troops followed their chief off to challenge Rufus, Margaret could lay no claim as wife or mother.

This was the way of their lives. Three times since Margaret and Malcolm had married, Malcolm had mounted a strong attack against William I. How many times had he defended against William's incursions? Season to season there were complaints of violation for Malcolm constantly to address, either by sword or by dove.

Strange this world was, in which Edith and David continued to correspond with their mother about life in William Rufus's gentle court, while Malcolm and their other sons rode out to fend him off. How these things grew into one's skin, so that you carried them with steady strength and with steady fatigue! Even all the delights of each day, from her children and from all the people and beauties Margaret loved, were all one in this steady work of her life, which she prayed that Jesus carried. It was as if she had jumped into a roaring spate and swam or floated or fought so wholly that appreciating was not separate from doing.

Margaret was thankful each time her husband and sons returned, delighted in them while she had them, and, whether they were with her or not, lived for them and for her countrymen in the ways she was used to, and in ways newly inspired.

25

When Malcolm left for Alnwick with their older sons, Margaret could not go out to bid them farewell. For now half a year, this flickering sickness had held her to her bed. At first, when one day she could not get up and move about, she would rest hard and look forward to the freshness of the next morning, when she would feel stronger. The days when she could be active promised growth in health, until work would be not always so dragging. But mornings when she could rise grew fewer and fewer. She had thought the sun and brightness of summer would help to dry the evil mold within her, but even the birdsong, the song of people in the fields, the dappling of light, and the lightness of air seemed to leave her behind. She felt instead the smothering heat that made infection swell and suppurate. This weakness, this dizzy squeamishness, sometimes with fever and sometimes not, would not abate. The coolness of fall brought relief, but as days grew shorter she felt the life waning all around her and dreaded the months ahead.

Malcolm had returned from his autumn trip to Carlisle to pay homage to William Rufus, grim with heavy purpose. How William had humiliated him at Carlisle was unspeakable. It left no room for interpretation. If Malcolm did not move back upon them with all the force he could find, William would be cutting his black swath up into Scotland, as he had desolated North Umbria.

Before it could grow a day colder, they must send out the call to all who loved Scotland's peace to come to fight or to bring supplies for so many men.

The day Margaret heard that the army was ready, she had asked her ladies to help her clean her teeth and wash, and to put on a fresh shift. She had meant to dress withal, and walk on Malcolm's arm out to the departing company—to press her head to each horse's head and speak gentle words in his ear, and to embrace her husband and her sons with sure peace. But hardly had she trembled into her shift when she found herself flat on the bed, asking the women to leave her a little, and then call Malcolm to come to her. Could she but still the trembling? Could she find steel in herself to give him when he came?

Handing herself over to Christ and his strength, she did embrace each of her sons firmly in blessing from her bed. But when Malcolm lifted her to his chest, she, pale and smelling of sickness, who should be his strength, broke to sobbing with rolling tears, and she could not stop. Her sons, mercifully, made their way out, and her husband held her tight as long as she sobbed and after, until she was still and they were silent together.

There could be no words, no attempts of their own. Except that when at last he laid her back on the pillows, she traced the Cross on his forehead, and he on hers. Then he left so quietly, and she stayed quiet.

She heard the sounds of the whole company starting down the road, but they seemed very far away. She closed her eyes so that those moving about her room would treat her as if she slept.

Malcolm's arms, hard now with the strength of age, and his steady great heart, had so many times warmed her into her own strength. She had often felt satisfied, too, that he left her embrace newly whole. But the grief now was that though he held her strongly, he could give her no strength. She had not the substance in her that could receive it. And she could give him *nothing!* It was as if a dried up umbilical cord lay at their feet. Darker sorrow was the pull in her to leave it that way. Did she want anything more than to roll away and be left alone?

No use to worry about these things. Rest. Rest in God. Jesus has done this. This is the time when very little is up to me.

But the tears ran. Her daughter Edith was scolding her:

"You drink almost nothing, Mother, and your fever rises. You can't lose tears! You'll make it worse! You can be sad, Mother, but do not cry!"

The blackness she knew whenever war was near sweltered about her. What good would the siege do? Would it relieve anyone from suffering or make anyone free? Where hid the mindless warrior's vanity? And the wave that followed this siege ... How long until they themselves heard the shouts of attack at their walls, their poor country folk gathered in for shelter?

Malcolm was nearly seventy years old—older than a warrior ever expected to be. (Does a sword slice any harder through a tough old body than through one oiled with youth?) His reflexes were not as quick; his endurance not so great. Even his judgment was not so arrow-sharp and quick.

Margaret had long made habit of trusting these things to her husband. She did not understand statecraft; she did not sympathize with the need to fight. She accepted that there was much she could not understand, and that, aside from understanding, the choice to make war was not hers. She could give her husband and her people such love and peace that they would not hanker to fight. When they did fight, she could send them with strong love, Christ's love, to lift them above the berserk.

This time of lying weak in bed was a time of habit more than consciousness. Margaret experienced general stifling—blackness enveloping the impotence she knew whenever she thought.

They had moved her into a little room just off the castle hall so she would not be disturbed by the life that went on there. The doorway was usually left open to let in the warmth of the hall fire. In the wall that faced outside was a stone which could be removed for surveillance. How she loved that small window! Seldom would she let her serving folk put the stone back into place. The window opened out upon the whole countryside— indeed, Margaret felt, upon all of her Scotland.

From that window she rode with her husband and sons. She heard her people calling back and forth—sometimes with words they would blush to know their queen heard! She heard the sounds of the farmers plowing or threshing, of cart wheels bumping along; of a women's washing party returning from the river. She heard and smelled and even saw the creation that goes on doing God's bidding by nature: the sun warming and cleaning, riding on breezes; the winds of so many kinds, playful and light or in dead earnest, bearing water to drench the earth or snatching the water from the earth and blowing it dry; the waters letting themselves steadily down from the heavens or wildly thrashing the land; the water dripping in measure from the roof; the starlight in still, deep skies, and sometimes the moon like silver music; always, beneath all, the steady sound of the sea. She heard and smelled the animals, little and scuffling or great and clomping. The flat bleating of sheep carried sometimes on the air, the sound of being at home in Scotland. Most of all, the dear birds of the field sent her each his own melody, lifting her up and calling her to fly with them.

Edith said the window would be Margaret's death. "You are so cold," she said, "and we might keep it a little warmer in here without this constant draft!"

Margaret *was* cold. She could not get warm. Her hound, Blue, stayed with her night and day lying on her feet.

The days passed so long! Though her court meant to let her rest, they found one problem and another that only she could solve. Those dyeing a great batch of wool had left it too long and ruined it. St. Andrew's feast was approaching, and how were they to celebrate it with no fighting men here? The steward said this was no time to feast, with war threatening at their door. He was already trying to get in extra supplies and getting nowhere. Two of the maids were sabotaging each other, and so wrecking goods and peace that belonged to all. The man who usually oversaw the farms and buildings had gone to war, and his substitute was not respected. Those who were used to coming to be fed and cared for, and those who expected her to sit on her rock, had gifts and messages to convey to her, or they were not convinced that she was really ill. They wanted to see that she had not been kidnapped. Her daughter Edith might bring one person each day to see that she was really ill before he would accept help from another.

Daily came the messengers who were in touch with the king, and Bishop Turgot would come to discuss with Queen Margaret the threat, and the progress of activity.

The shameful thing was that she could not rouse interest in any of it. After twenty-five years of practice in love for her people, she wished not to hear their troubles. It was not only that she knew them to be well capable of caring for themselves, or that she trusted God would care for them. Where was her affection for them? It seemed harder to forget herself for them than it had been the first day she had tried it. She kept herself kind; she rose from the pillows for each guest. She listened and thought and conferred with the chaplain. But she wanted nothing but to sleep.

Toward her children she felt some interest, and Malcolm she longed for. All but those who had gone with Malcolm to battle were home now, since Margaret's state seemed so grave. One and then the other took a turn staying with her in the small room off the hall. How she could have endured if they had not? Whether it was Mary or Edith, or Edmund or Alexander or David, whenever she looked she would see one of them sitting quietly in the low light, doing hand work—wool or embroidery, or leather or arms or fish nets. Sometimes she would ask one to read to her. Sometimes they sang to her the songs they had often sung—merry lyrics and choruses, and the songs of God.

One day Margaret awoke to find that they must have brought in some guests while she was sleeping. Old women in their dark shawls huddled together over there in the corner, conferring. No, they were cooking. They had a small fire. The savor that came from the roasting meat was delicious. She was starving for it. No meat had smelled so true and good for such a long time! Was it roasted chicken?

The women basted it as it turned, and the juices hissed as it browned. Tender, it must be, and a little salty. Ah! Would her poor folk offer her this? This gift she would not refuse! They, with so little meat for themselves, would bring her meat that at last she could eat, dripping with juice. She must be careful to hold back. She felt she could tear off every piece to the bone.

One of the bent old women turned and hobbled toward her, extending in her hand a piece of meat. Margaret did not recognize her exactly. When had she seen her?

"Will you eat, my dear queen? Take it, dear lady, we have more. You have been savoring its smell, have you not?"

Margaret reached for the golden, succulent bit. Was it a leg? No, a wing. No, it had a curled, crisp little human hand!

"Yes, my dear, it's the arm of a babe! Brigid's babe! She gave it to us. But it's your baby to eat—you drove her to it! So harsh you were. Rules for everything! Your great hall stifled her, so she went to the hayloft for air. *There* she could laugh! *There* one would treat her sweetly and tell her she was beautiful!"

Margaret's tears came as if to pull out her insides.

"Brigid! Know you not I love you? Why couldn't you come to me? I would have taken your babe!"

"Ah, and here you have the babe. Sweet meat, dear Margaret. Eat before you go. Soon you'll be here no more. Throughout the land we'll all taste that sweet meat!"

The other two dark, lumpy forms had moved up to their sister, and their faces leered close with hers.

"The people wait for you to die, Margaret! They've missed us Three Sisters long enough. We'll not punish them. We've missed them, too. We'll let them take us in. Soon again we Three Weird Sisters will be joining every family round its pot."

"You aren't real!" Margaret cried, "Get out!"

"We aren't real? You're hungry, aren't you? You're starving for this tender flesh and bones."

Her cross. She lifted it to them, trying to distinguish them in the flashing colors of her vision.

"What are you doing, Mother? Do you think you're the holy Columkille preaching?"

It was Edith. She sat her up and jolted her around, wiped her face with a warm cloth, and pulled back her hair.

"There now, Mother, see where you are. There's no one to preach to but the dog. That's it—a queen with a dog upon her feet! Down, Blue, and out! Find someone stronger than yourself."

Edith held a hot drink to her mother's lips and Margaret made some go down her throat.

"You look flushed, Mother. I'll take away some of these robes. There. Sleep now, and don't disturb me again."

Edith settled herself by the light and took her distaff in hand. It was too dark in here to do fine work.

Margaret was cold. She could have used those robes, for sure. And now Blue was gone.

This I can do, she thought. *You did not say anything, Jesus. I think I can be quiet, too.*

"Bless you, dear Edith."

"Shush!"

Edith was the only one who could not settle peacefully. She often sent one of the others away, trusting no one but herself to do what was needed. She must always bring some new poultice. She pushed drinks to Margaret's lips, now hot and now cold. She conferred with wise wives and brought new brews for Margaret to drink meekly, things with hair balls floating on top, or small creatures dead at the bottom.

"What kind of black magic are you dealing with, daughter? I will not sip through hair!"

But it is true that Edith also brought the good broth from the black cattle, which warmed and made her able to drink at all. She it was who had found that if they boiled goat's milk, Margaret could drink.

Edith was the one who kept Margaret clean. The others thought to console her, but would probably have left her to her sweats. Edith scrubbed her and made her get up shivering while she changed the sheets and layered them with pungent herbs. She was forever oiling her. Lanolin was not so bad, but the fish oil made Margaret cry once her daughter had left the room.

Constantly, as she worked, Edith preached. She had gossip to convey, always with a moral. She berated her mother for losing her spirit.

"Our father takes his life in his hands moment by moment. He sleeps on the rocks with one hand on his weapon, and without even a fire or a warm drink. He carries the hearts of all his men and rises to their needs. *There* is a man who has given himself to God! Haven't you taught us, Mother, that if we but give ourselves to God, we will do more than they say of any of the gods of old—in spite of ourselves?

"But you, Mother, you lie clutching the covers in this dark closet waiting for me to change your sheets. You will not eat; you will not walk. If you but got up and walked twice around the hall, and tomorrow twice around the courtyard, you'd soon be walking evenly, with your head held high. If you would but dress beautifully again and go sit with people—maybe not yet to serve, but to hold the babies and listen to the wives talk—spirit would come back to the people. And maybe you would start to *care* about them.

"We are at the edge of a great chasm, Mother, and you were crowned our queen! You are but forty-seven years of age, Mother. How do you satisfy yourself that you can rest?"

At last Margaret asked Edith to read to her.

Edith took up the Book of Job, and began to read the harangues of his friends. Margaret stopped her.

"Kind Edith, I have heard enough of men talking to men. Read me the Canticle of Canticles."

"Mother, your heart cannot take such fierce passion. And the book speaks of death."

She paged seriously through the great book and paused. "Ah, here is a song of love between God and man," and she began to read the Lamentations of Jeremiah.

Now, though Margaret would have asked only the relief of silence, she could not lie in silence with those moaning dirges resting on her chest.

"Let me ask you, dear daughter. Would you lead me with a letter of St. John? I think I can pray them from memory if you will only strengthen me with your voice."

Dutifully, Edith began to read. She came to the words, "He who says he loves God but hates his brother is a liar." With these she stopped.

"Mother, you must sleep now. I'll get some men to put this stone back. The evil night air is settling on your bed."

With the stone replaced in the window space, Margaret could not even see where Edith sat, and the room was indeed quiet. She watched the play of red from the hall fire on the black wall. She closed her eyes, and great splashes of red like iron in the forge shimmered and bounced under her eyelids. Yellow flashes and sparks cascaded across. The colors pulsed in her hot body. Margaret rode along on these lights and flashes as long as she could stand, and sat up. Trembling, she put her feet over the side of the bed and felt for the cold stone floor. She reached for the ale flask. She must have a cool drink. She must drink all she could. Though her hands shook so and the flask seemed heavy, she did drink deep.

Pivoting so softly back to her pillows, she smiled with satisfaction. *I guess I can drink, aye, Edith? Aye, and never wake you!* she thought.

She could not stop her shivering, fighting those lights inside her eyes.

A hunched, black figure moved silently through the doorway. Was it one of her poor old women? The woman came close to her, lifted her hood, and brought her face to Margaret's face. Yes, it was Ebba, who had come so often, and who had said the ale was sour and the meat was all gristle. It was she who had accused Margaret of wearing simple dresses when she was with the poor so that she could save her silks and satins from vermin. She had dared Margaret to deny that in all her giving to the poor and downtrodden she was but flaunting her name.

"Aye, you're always bending down to us," she had said. "Low, where you keep us! Aye, you love to give so that all the land says, 'Oh, Queen Margaret, Mother of Gifts!' But will you *take* from the poor? Will *you* eat *our* poor scraps in our own dark huts? Oh, no, not you! You're pure as the driven snow! You cannot drag your gown in the scummy swamp!"

That was the day Margaret had gone down with the woman to the tiny thatched pile of stones where she lived. And truly, the dinner had been a hard one to eat.

Now the old lady's face breathed in hers.

"Liar!

"Liar!

"Say the truth that you know! You hate me! You have never loved me and you can't! Try again to push those sweet words out, that whatever you do to me you do to the Holy One! You, always scrounging for the ugly and the runts. You know who we are, and we're not holy. We're *ugly*, see! Who's ugly? You *know* who's ugly. The ugly come from hell!"

Her eyes glowed red. She drew her long, claw-like fingernails in two furrows down her face, releasing a pussy, running serum. She reached with the same nails and scratched from Margaret's forehead down through her eyes and to her jawbone.

"You've never loved the ugly, and we the ugly hate you! We have you, too! All your sweet advances, and you've made your friends, alright! We await you in hell!"

Margaret reached for the woman's hands.

They were not there. Only the black darkness was there, shimmering red with green edges.

It was so still.

They were but air. But they came from her mind! The evil of ugliness—Margaret knew that Christ had conquered it. In that she did not waver. But she *was* a liar! She did hate to be with the ugly, no matter how she tried to love.

Somewhere near her must be the black cross. It was the one she had often gazed upon to help her pray, and now she kept it with her in bed. Not thinking in words, she had the idea: *If I kiss this, do I betray you?*

Oh Lord, have mercy, I must kiss your cross.

She clutched it, shivering, grateful to her Lord that he would let her grip his cross, liar or not.

So went the nights. She would lie on her left side, but it gave her pain. She turned to the right and began to twitch. She wanted to lie prone, but could not well turn her head to either side. Lying, the bed swirled; but to rise made it worse. Best seemed to be slightly sitting, raised on pillows.

Her whole body often clenched in pain, and her teeth sang. She thirsted, but even water smelled bad. The slightest disturbance would start her to cough. The cough would rack her, mounting until blood spewed out, and still it would not stop. The calming teas they gave her, and the heating poultices, did little but to assuage those who tended her.

Dawn must be near, she would think, and see that Edith was still with her. Alexander had not yet come, and he came faithfully at eleven o'clock at night. *Oh, if eternity be longer than these nights, God save every man from hell!*

The hours of laboring with child; those of sitting with little Ethelrede, or small Malcolm, or Donald as they fought for life; the hours of watching, waiting for her husband's embrace when he would come from battle: those hours had not been as long as the hours of one of these nights. Not so long had been the nights when cares threatened them gravely, or when Malcolm must fight within himself. Then she would lie in his arms listening, or sit up in bed with candle lit, to consider and to plot, and to write it down. Those nights, worry had no seeming answer; or Margaret may have come to her answer, but Malcolm had not come to his. He would go over and over the same problems and angers while she listened and comforted, thinking how soon the babe must nurse, and then how soon she must be up to start the next day.

Not even so long had been those nights after Malcolm may have made little of her, overbore her, or smugly ignored her, and then happily flopped on the bed and slept like a bear. Those nights she had curled tightly on her side of the bed and marveled that he would not have known if she shook the bed with sobs.

Then, thinking of all the duties coming so soon in the morning, she would ask her Blessed Mother Mary,

Please, dear Lady, set me free. Let me sleep forgiveness. If he can sleep thus, then it must be right for me to sleep, too.

Those were the nights when sleep was like vinegar, leaving her shriveled and sour in the morning.

How could these nights be longer?

It was one of these nights, as the sounds of the hall seemed to have settled, that Margaret heard a rustle in the doorway, and beheld such a great bearded face, helmeted and painted for war. Noiselessly he moved toward her, until he stood very near. Other huge, painted warriors kept silently coming after him. They bore burning pine knots, lighting their greasy features and their heavy, smutty armor. No sound would come from her throat. She could not even look away as they leered at her. Were they Norsemen? No, their blue and ochre paint was that of the ancient Picts. Nothing else could she recognize about their dress.

The men began to hack the beams with their great war axes, and they broke the wall separating her room from the hall, swinging sword and morning star. Why were they soundless? Now they had moved away from her into the hall's dimness. Sleepers were lifted and hurled, children and women screamed, groggy men and women swung swords or hurled whatever was at hand. She heard the knocking of heads and the cracking of bones; she could recognize no one in the tumbling havoc.

They had hold of someone—a man. No, a young boy. They had all converged on him, tearing off his clothes. They were pinning him spread eagle on the floor. She saw his face. David!

Margaret jumped or stumbled from the bed and fell upon the first brute she could reach. She fell straight through his body to the rough floor, and lay sobbing, "David! David!"

"David! David!"

"Mother, come." It was Mary, lifting her gently to her lap, there on the floor in the darkness. She pulled her mother close and rocked her softly like an injured child.

"Did you dream, Mother? I am here."

"Where is David? Bring him, Mary, will you please?"

They had her again in bed when she saw his form in the doorway, black in front of the hall's firelight. Yes, the doorway. The wall was still there! Was this really he?

He came toward her into the lantern light. Oh, how he was like his namesake, "A youth ruddy, and comely to behold." He had on only what he slept in, and how vulnerable he looked, wiry and young.

"Come and hold me, David!"

When he took her in his arms, she would not let go, until she felt she must smother. Then she asked him to stay. She couldn't seem to breathe, and could he put on warm clothes and hold her up for just awhile?

And so David got up on the bed and sat against the wall with his mother cradled against his chest, the furs pulled up close around them, and bore her through the hours. It was the first peace she had known for some days. The joy, the pride she took in his tender strength! Aye, he was still willowy, but already a man. He would so comfort some wife. He was crooning to her. This squire who clanked around with horses and arms was humming her the lullaby she had hummed to him. It was one of the sad, caressing songs she had first heard in Scotland, one she often sang to God. Margaret drifted off to sleep, forgetting to worry whether her son would leave.

Indeed he did not leave. In the bright sun of morning he had but slipped a bit on the pillows his sister had stuffed under him when she had come to take her watch.

Many nights after that David held her in the same way. When he did, Margaret could pray for him without fear. She wanted to protect him. Why was it that his very protecting her consoled her? It was he, her youngest son, for whom she felt most fear. He was thirteen. So much could he still learn from a mother. So much could he still grow from a mother's faith in him, before his back had hardened and his skin had toughened for the burdens of a man!

She knew, too, that someday he must lead. Either here or across the sea, he must be good enough to bring good to a whole people, God help him! Would his brothers help him? It would be easy to get pinched among them. Had they risen at all above the murderous jealousy their father had avenged before their country could live at peace? Ah, with Malcolm he would be protected. Malcolm would guard them all into maturity.

Yes, if she could hang on until Malcolm returned. Margaret felt no strength now to lean out for life. She knew death was tight on top of her. She could hold it off, though, until again she could rest in Malcolm's arms. Only his arms, and then she could leave.

She waited each day for Bishop Turgot to give her Communion, for the moment she could bond with the only One who gave meaning. Soon she must be seeing him, and herself, and all she loved as God sees them! Yet she felt nothing.

You are here, she affirmed. *I am coming to you. You, the Lord of the universe, are within me. The universe, Lord. You hold it. You are within me—and I sense it not at all!*

One morning Margaret awoke clearheaded. The sun came warm through her little window. Some kind of large assembly was outside. She rose and put on a tunic over her shift, belted it, and put on her shoes. She walked out into the hall and through the great entrance doors. She was strong and sure, and she could breathe the pure air well.

The crowds were not in the courtyard, but over on the village green, by the church. She walked across the drawbridge and toward the crowd. Folk were laughing and dancing, young and old. It was the ancient Druidic spring dance.

But this was Sunday!

"Come!" she urged the fine, strong wife closest to her. "This is not the dance for today! It's Sunday! The Lord's Supper is in church! Wash your face and come!"

The woman only kept up her dancing. Her sweat was hot and old on the air.

Margaret went to another, and then to another, but all ignored her. At last, she took a small child by the hand and began to lead him toward the church. The child's gaunt father came up close to her face, hissed, and snatched away the child.

Margaret pushed her way to the church and leaned against its door. It moved open to let her in. The church, too, was crowded. But what was that up on the altar? Some bloody mess, with a circle of fine, light-footed dancers twirling round the altar. Who was that noble, tall man leaping so high and turning one flimsy maiden and then another to him and away? Malcolm! How high he leaped, and how he would pull a girl to him, drawing her up along his leg.

When he had swung one aside, he drew near the altar, peering at whatever carcass it was lying on the altar. He dipped his forefinger into its blood and came so quietly, so gracefully, so *shamelessly*, as a leopard would come, right up to her face, and touched his bloody finger to her forehead. He brought his face to hers and covered her mouth with his great, wet lips and kissed her—kissed her until he had drawn out all her breath, and still sucked from her lips. She struggled loose enough to draw in a great gasp of air.

"Malcolm! Malcolm! Why, Malcolm?" She crumpled at his feet, breathing great sobs.

How long Margaret kept her face in her hands and her knees drawn to her face she did not know. At last, so tired, she reached her hand a little out on the floor. It was not the floor, it was her sheets. She lifted her eyes only a little. She was only here on the bed, and dawn had not come.

She sobbed all the day. Her Malcolm! When must he come? He *was* true, she knew it. If only he could hold her! Even though that be a dream, if only he could hold her!

She gripped her black cross. Never until these days had she thought how her Lord was not able to grip his cross. No one to hold him, and he could hold no one. Jesus could hold no thing, not even his cross, he who was pinned open to empty himself.

Was she praying or not? She was so tired, and always there were those red and green flickerings and explosions on black.

I do love you, she whispered. *Let me hold you. Let me hold you. Have mercy on me, Lord Jesus Christ, Son of God! I am a sinner!*

The nights and days passed one into another. One night, far into the watches, Margaret woke to see the Three Sisters again, dancing up to her in the dark like footless puppets.

"Run!" they cried. "Run for your life! Save them all! Everyone is running!"

They grabbed and pulled Margaret out of bed and across the floor. Somehow fear gave her strength, and she ran with them. They burst through the great hall doors and stood on the edge of a flimsy pier extending into a boiling gray sea. Others crowded them, pushing her so that she knew she must fall. Curraghs and other small, light boats bobbed about in the sea, each filled with people. There were larger boats, too, barely above water for the loads of people they carried. Some of the boats bobbed toward the pier, and the people with her yelled out to them and threw themselves into them if they came close enough. Those in the boats tried only to get away. They paddled madly, but no one would match with anyone else, so that they moved aimlessly. If one of those who cast himself from the pier missed a boat, the rowers struck out with their oars, whapping them until their heads rose no more.

"Jump!" yelled the Sisters.

She seemed to fly on their shoulders until she slapped into the bottom of a boat. Two of the old Sisters touched water, but like child faeries, somehow came to be crowded in with her.

"What is happening?" Margaret cried to the boatload of people now thumping into them. Her voice was not at all lost in the storm.

"It's the great flood!" the man in the neighboring boat yelled back, he also easy to hear in spite of the storm. "He's going to let the sea loose. We've got to get out! We've got to get out!"

"Where are we going?" she cried.

"We've got to get out! We've got to get out!"

Every person in every boat they approached she recognized. All were her people. She had held this child on her lap; listened to that one read. There was the woman who'd come to her at the rock, in great fear of her husband. Malcolm had taken that man by his side, and that woman had seemed so happy last time she saw her. Here were some of the serving folk; there the old priest from far north. They were all terrified and angry, screaming at one another, but never answering one another. Each worked with all his might to push or paddle, but every one was pushing against the others.

"Who knows where to go?" she called. "Who is leading us?"

Her voice was lost.

Then she saw the black shiny head towering above her. The back of her head touched her back as she looked up to a living dragon eyeing her from far above. The head moved in sickening great arcs as that huge neck swayed side to side. His black, shining back rose ten feet above the water, snaking out as far as she could see. The monster was just as people had told her dwelt in Loch Ness, only more huge, vastly more huge.

"He holds back the sea!" people cried. "If he lets go, we perish!"

Who was that in the boat beyond the next one? He was standing unafraid, as only Malcolm would. When his boat turned a little, she could see his face. He was gazing out as she had so often seen him gazing, a sure father upon his assembled clans. Yes, and the people were looking to him!

But yet he seemed not to be looking toward any of them. He seemed to be looking at nothing. He was directly facing her now, and she was waving at him, but he showed no recognition. The great, black head curved over him like a tidal wave.

"Mael Colum!" she called. "Mael Colum! Dear one!"

Was he even alive?

"Stop him, Mael Colum! You must kill him! You can! You can save us!"

He did seem to have heard her. His hand went to his sword and he looked up at the dragon's face—not with the determination of battle, but with dreamlike reflectiveness. He did nothing.

Again and again Margaret called to him. Would no one join her? Would no one help him?

Her boat, his boat, and all the others continually rose and fell, almost capsizing in the violent sea. The currents pushed her quite near to Malcolm, and she was sure he was looking at her.

"Kill him, Malcolm!" she shrieked.

Malcolm's face was so bland, and when he opened his mouth he stuttered.

"No. Kill, I cannot! No more!"

The great head came down and engulfed him. The great back rose, all the way to the tail looping miles into the sky. As it rose and flew free of the water, the water, which it had held back, rushed forward, swelling toward a great drop. Like flotsam were the little crafts full of people, falling together and swirling apart, paddles striking out into air, voices lost in the turbulence.

Boat after boat disappeared over the falls. Then, Margaret, too, was tumbling in nothingness. Far below was red, roaring fire. The Weird Sisters floated close to her, now one, now another.

"You can't come back!" each one would screech. "You can't come back!"

"You can't come back!" all of those falling with her were calling. They called not in a chorus, but in a thousand contending tones: "You can't come back!"

Margaret heard herself whispering in the darkness, "I can't come back."

The darkness was still, cold, and hard. The bed was firm under her. No one was with her, and the fire in the hall must be very low, for she could see no light on the walls.

26

It was one afternoon when drafts of mellow sun came in through her window. Margaret heard the horses and jangling equipment passing through the gate. She heard the clank of mail across the hall and turned her head toward the doorway. Edgar stood there—her son. He was all white and gray, poised in dismay, as if to jump from a high rock. He took a step toward her and wavered. He continued toward her and dropped to kneel and clutch her shoulders, sobbing a man's terrible sobs.

She could not hold him, but she rested her arms on his.

"It's both of them, Mother! Morel, mormaer to Robert de Moubray, fell on Father. Father died there. They're trying to get his body, but where they'll take it, I don't know, for Donald Bane is coming with many a chief and men. He must have been waiting to hear.

"Edward fell, too, Mother. They took him. He can't still be alive. It was a deadly wound!"

Long moments passed before she grabbed his hair and raised his head. She looked into his eyes. Where was her mother's strength? Where was her soft, strong voice of peace? She opened her mouth to give him comfort, but no voice came. She gazed at him mute, clinging to his hair.

"We have nothing, Mother. Donald Bane's army marches here now."

Now, if only she could hold on for the skirling that brought them back home! Donald must let them bring his own brother home. If she could see Mael Colum's face, however it may be! If Mael Colum could not hold her, then if she, at least, could hold him.

Nay, if she could live even after she had held him …

Jesus, shall I stay? Will you raise me?

David. The House of Dunkeld.

The house is full of people, and so little to feed them. Can I save them from ruin, Lord?

I can. I can speak peace. Donald will listen to me. I have been tired, but give me strength and I'll take it. I can!

But it was as if a vein had been cut and her lifeblood flowed out on the floor. She could barely raise herself or follow thought.

Is my life going, Jesus? You give me leave to let them go?

This silence, this iron void, was like nothing that had ever surrounded her.

Bishop Lanfranc's promise from the long years ago when she had found her call lay softly in her heart:

"Do not worry, Margaret. You want to give yourself to God alone. He will let you. Some he asks to declare themselves all his at the start. You he will strip day by day, until you can give yourself to him naked and alone, as he gave himself to you."

At first the sounds might not have been sounds. Had they been there before but noticed only now? Then they became sure and clear—a wild pulse of drums, pipes, and confused clangor; human voices riding the wind, ululating and screeching as from hell itself. They grew ever louder until they bore right against the walls.

Margaret rubbed her face and pulled herself up, squeezed her eyes open and shut, and focused on her little window. Not another dream! But the cries of Highland warriors did not diminish.

"Donald Bane is here," she heard.

The folk from round about had gathered within the castle walls during this last night, and for now were safe. But when Donald Bane would break through, it would be the end of the sons of Malcolm. Long enough had he burned with his purpose. It was to wipe clean the house he called defiled.

Then fog came down on Edinburgh Castle, and on all the country round. It lay so thick that though the armies camped close around the castle, they withheld siege. Still, they clenched the castle tightly guarded. No one entered or left except by secret ways.

No sound came from the enemy. Even the sounds of life from all those taking refuge in courtyard and hall were subdued—an occasional call from the watch; once in awhile shouts or raised voices—all sounds dropped in the fog.

Bishop Turgot was here now all the time. Dear man he was, so often at cross-wills with Margaret during these years, yet ever generous and faithful. He read her the Church's prayers. Her sons and daughters took their turns reading them, too. In her black and colorful flickering, Margaret clung to the words. Sometimes they buzzed in her ears, echoing and shouting until she almost rose out of bed. She would grasp her black cross. When she could not bear sound, those who waited with her gave her silence. But then the silence, too, would buzz, and she would reach for whoever was near, and they could not hold her tight enough.

Today again, they waited.

"Father," Margaret said, "Has it been long enough since the last time I received the Lord?"

144

"Aye, I think it has," answered Bishop Turgot, and rose to leave for the Sacrament.

"Father, hear my sins," she raised her voice. "Come and reconcile me."

The priest knelt on the stone floor by her bed and all moved away to leave them alone. Some had gone to get all the family to be here for Margaret's Communion.

When Turgot returned from the chapel, Margaret's lips were forming the words as they had silently followed the priest's each day at Mass:

"Lord, Jesus Christ, Son of the living God," she prayed, "who, by the Father's will and the cooperation of the Holy Spirit ..."

All were praying with her now, for they all knew the words. They were not leading, as often with the sick who are carried along, skipping and stumbling, by the strong words of the healthy. All looked to Margaret and followed her. Her prayer was labored, one phrase at a time, but it was steady, carried by her heart:

> "...through your death brought life to the world,
> deliver me by this, your most sacred Body and Blood,
> from all my sins
> and from every evil.
> Make me always obedient to your commandments,
> and never
> allow me to be parted from you;
> who lives
> and rules
> with the same God the Father
> and the Holy Spirit,
> one God
> forever and ever.
> Amen.

"O Lord, Jesus Christ,
let not the partaking of your Body,
which I,
unworthy as I am,
make bold to receive,
turn against me into a judgment and condemnation,
but through your loving kindness
let it be for me
a safeguard and healing remedy, both of mind and
body;
who lives and rules with God the Father in the unity
of the Holy Spirit, one God
forever
and ever.
Amen."

The bishop came now. Margaret's almost worthless mouth took the thin, white disc and managed to swallow it. No one watched to see if she could. Not even Edith fussed around her face, for all were living in their hearts with her in her heart, receiving her hidden King.

Still, Margaret felt nothing.

Then young Mary glanced up and saw her mother motion to her. She came close and knelt, and Margaret traced a cross on her forehead. After Mary rose, Margaret motioned to David, he came, and, in like manner, each of Margaret and Malcolm's sons and daughters took their turn. They would each remember all their lives Margaret's thumb on their foreheads—not trembling and clammy with illness, but firm with a loving purpose. They would still feel that blessing, and her reaching to them from where she was. Some who watched had seen, in the thick of battle, a mortally wounded warrior completing great deeds long after blood and strength had left. Margaret's acts of blessing put them in mind of this.

They held her up to help her draw air into her lungs.

Now some began to stir to return to the state of things in the castle, conferring on who would stay with their mother.

Then came a breathless, heaven-touched stillness. It was the stillness that had filled the birth room each time they had told her that they could see her child's head. Someone was coming, Someone who had been with her these many months, but who was now going to show his face.

Margaret still labored. She gripped her black cross as she had gripped the arms of her two midwives those other wondrous times. It would not be long. He was almost here.

Epilogue

The mist that had first embraced Margaret into Scotland now safely wrapped the small party that slipped out of Edinburgh castle and past Donalbane's watch, carrying her body to be laid to rest next to Malcolm's at Dunfermline Abbey.

The pale Donald did capture Edinburgh, but had not held it a year when Duncan took it back. As the Normans made steady inroads, the reign of Scotland stayed in the hands of the sons of Margaret and Malcolm. David became king in 1124, and for thirty years cultivated what his mother had begun, with substantial innovation, market development, and confirmation in the Catholic Faith. He was to be declared a saint by the Catholic Church.

Other sons and daughters of Margaret and Malcolm paired with royal families in Europe, some to rule well, some less well. Maud (Edith) actually married a son of William the Conqueror, Henry I of England. Thus an Atheling again reigned over that land. When Stephen of Blois seized kingship for himself, their daughter, Holy Roman Empress Maud, became famous for her interminable, ruinous war against him. Edmond, called "The Monk" proved himself so treacherous that, by an unfortunate disciplinary custom of the time, he was banished to a monastery, where he in turn could punish the monks for the rest of his life.

Queen Margaret is said to have set Scotland on "the happiest two hundred years of her history." Some, from her time until now, say that the tall, copper-haired Atheling emasculated the clans and the ancient Scottish ways. They say that she suffocated them with the effete ways of the Continent; with the bonds of the Pale Galilean. But few will deny that in that two hundred years, a Scotsman was most likely to be able to lie down each night peacefully with his family, not doubting that house and crops and livestock would be there whole in the morning. He could arise to find each day the markets busy and full of new things. He would be able to learn to read. He would be able to make and to do things better than ever before.

What Margaret had hoped to do was not to smother, but to transform the good she found. Among the emerging nations, could Scotland have carried herself without the momentum Queen Margaret set rolling?

The hundreds of places in Scotland still named for her after nine hundred years tell of love. For whether or not she brought the customs of Christendom, what she brought was a heart for each man, woman, and child as though that person were the only one. She brought a heart fearless of the evilest spirits, spirits that brought steely chieftains cowering to the ground. And she brought such an onslaught for her Great Laird as to free every chief and every child for the courage and love of life that come only from God.

In 1250 Pope Innocent IV used that preposterous power the Catholic Church claims from Christ to declare Margaret, Queen of Scotland, a Saint—a woman absolutely fulfilled, a woman to learn from, a woman alive and to be counted on for love. For what greater fulfillment is there than to make real all that was planted in her soul, and to become one with the great Lord of the Universe and of the Cross, carrying so many others with her to that place where none need restrain their love?

In 1673, the Church named St. Margaret patron of Scotland. Her feast day is celebrated on November 16.

May Edgar and Edith-Matilda-Maud forgive me for portraying them somewhat unfavorably. I could learn little of the personalities of Margaret's brother and sister and children. She must have had someone like each of these two in her life, and how can her true self be shown without them?

Sources Quoted

McGinley, Phyllis, <u>Saint-Watching</u>. (Viking Press, 1969)

Menzies, Lucy; Knox, Ronald; Wright, Ronald Selby (edited by Charles Robertson), <u>St. Margaret, Queen of Scotland, and her Chapel</u>. (St. Margaret's Chapel Guild; Inglis Allen, 1994)

Turgot, <u>The Life of St. Margaret, Queen of Scotland</u>. (St. Margaret's Catholic Church, Dunfermline, 1993)